CLAIMED FOR MAKAROV'S BABY

CLAIMED FOR MAKAROV'S BABY

BY

SHARON KENDRICK

First published in Great Britain 2015
By Mills & Boon, an imprint of HarperCollins*Publishers*
1 London Bridge Street, London, SE1 9GF

Large Print edition 2016

© 2015 Sharon Kendrick

ISBN: 978-0-263-26151-6

Our policy is to use papers that are natural, renewable and recyclable products and made from wood grown in sustainable forests. The logging and manufacturing processes conform to the legal environmental regulations of the country of origin.

Printed and bound in Great Britain
by CPI Antony Rowe, Chippenham, Wiltshire

To Paul Newrick—
who is not only completely charming,
but positively *encyclopaedic*
when it comes to the subject of planes,
and who has helped me with air transport
for many of my billionaire heroes!

And also to Michela Sanges,
whose knowledge of all things Russian
is inspirational.

CHAPTER ONE

IT DIDN'T MEAN ANYTHING. It was just a means to an end. A few words and a signature on a piece of paper and then afterwards...

Erin swallowed as the silky white dress brushed against her bare ankles. Afterwards she would be able to create a better future. A different kind of future. Most of all, she would be secure—and wasn't that the whole point of this? That she would be *safe*.

But she could feel her palms growing clammy as she clutched the bouquet of flowers her groom had insisted she buy—'It will add authenticity...'—and wondered if her bright, forced smile would add the same kind of authenticity. She doubted it. As she walked towards the registrar's desk her face was reflected back in a mirror—a face almost as white as her dress. Beside her stood a man—a kind man and a dear friend whom she must pretend to love, at least until the ceremony was over. And that was the hardest part of all.

Because she didn't believe in love. She'd tried it once and it had only reinforced what she'd already known. That love was for fools, and hadn't she been the biggest one of all? She'd picked the worst kind of man. A man who was not worthy of love.

Of anyone's love.

The two witnesses were sitting quietly and the registrar was smiling, too, but Erin was certain she could see suspicion in the smart middle-aged woman's eyes. Did she guess? Did she have any kind of inkling that Erin Turner was about to break the law for the first time in her life?

Beside her, Chico reached out and curled his fingers around her wrist, giving it a comforting squeeze as the registrar began to speak.

'You are here to witness the joining in matrimony of Chico and Erin…'

There was a pause as Erin heard a door behind her open and the sound of footsteps, but her heart was thumping too loudly to care who had just walked in. Her smile felt as brittle as glass. Her hand was now so slippery that she was afraid of dropping the flowers. And then the question was being asked. The question she had practised not reacting to over and over again.

'If any person present knows of any lawful impediment to this marriage, he or she should declare it now.'

She watched the registrar give a quick nod—as if this particular query always got the same silent response—when suddenly a voice shattered the quiet of the institutional room.

'*Da.* I do.'

For a split second Erin froze and then she whirled round as she heard the Russian accent, her head refusing to believe what her heart and her body were telling her. That it was nothing but a mistake—a mistake with especially bad timing.

And then she was caught and captured—lasered by the brilliance of a pair of icy blue eyes—and Erin's heart plummeted, for this was no mistake. This was real. As real as the silk flowers which stood on the registrar's desk. As real as the sudden thunder of blood to her heart. Like a fizzing firework thrown into the blackest night, Dimitri Makarov was dominating the room with his unique blend of sex appeal and power, just as he always did.

Her fingers bit into the fleshy stems of her flowers as she stared at him. He was wearing a silvery-grey suit which emphasised his powerful build, and the artificial light from the cheap chandelier had turned his hair to molten gold. Prestige and privilege pulsated from every pore of his muscular body as he flicked his icy gaze over her.

But something about him was different. Gone was the bloodshot glow which had sometimes marred the beauty of those spectacular eyes. And gone, too, was the faint stubble which had habitually darkened his jaw and made him look slightly disreputable. This man was clean-shaven and his eyes were bright and clear and...*penetrating*.

'Dimitri,' Erin breathed.

'*Da*. The very same,' he said, his voice mocking her, but the look on his face sent a shiver down her spine. 'Pleased to see me, Erin?'

He knows, thought Erin.

He knows.

She told herself that he couldn't possibly know. It was over six years since she'd last seen him, when he'd made it clear how little she had meant to him. His attitude towards her had been insulting and dismissive—reminding her all too clearly that she'd only ever been a minion in his life. Somebody he could just shove aside when she got too close. And that was what had happened, wasn't it? She'd got way too close.

She thought of Leo and why she was here. Of everything she was fighting for, and she forced a smile onto her lips. Because if she showed the slightest sign of weakness, Dimitri would leap on it.

And devour her.

'This is rather bad timing,' she said lightly.

'I disagree. The timing could not have been better.'

'I'm just about to get married, Dimitri. To Chico.'

'I don't think so.' His gaze flicked over Chico, who was standing with his mouth gaping open and a distinct look of alarm in his eyes.

'Is there a problem?' asked the registrar pleasantly, but Erin could see her glancing at the telephone which sat on the desk beside the silk flowers, as if convincing herself that a line to the outside world lay within easy reach.

'A problem of a purely emotional nature,' answered Dimitri smoothly as he began to walk towards Erin.

Erin stiffened as he closed the space between them and even as her body started going into some sort of automatic meltdown at his approach the irony of his words did not escape her. Was Dimitri Makarov really claiming something to be of an *emotional nature*—when he was about as familiar with emotion as a shark was to sitting around a fire and warming its fin?

'Miss Turner?' said the registrar, fixing Erin with a questioning look, as if she was eager for the unexpected floor show to be over.

But it wasn't over. It was nowhere near over. Because Dimitri had now reached her and his tall shadow was enveloping her, like a stifling cloud which seemed to have sucked all the air from her lungs. She told herself to stop him— to scream out her protest or shove at that broad chest with one indignant hand—but she seemed powerless to do anything. And suddenly it was too late, because he was pulling her against him and his hands were wrapped around her back as he held her close. Trapped against his body, she could feel his fingers imprinting themselves on the thin silk of her wedding dress and it felt as if he were touching her bare skin. With a shuddered breath she lifted her face to his, to the icy glitter of his eyes, which studied her for a long moment before he bent his head to kiss her.

Erin could sense the contempt underpinning his action, but that didn't stop her lips from opening automatically beneath his, or her body starting to tremble the moment he touched her. Weakly, she recognised that this was not a kiss driven by affection or lust, but a mark of possession—a stamp of ownership. Yet it was a kiss too potent to resist and stupidly—even now—it made her start longing for the things she was never going to have.

He was pulling her closer, bringing her up against the proud jut of his hips and the unmistakable hardness at their centre, which was hidden from everyone in the room but her. She thought how...*outrageous* it was for him to push his erection against her quite so blatantly when there were other people around, but that didn't stop her from reacting to it, did it—from wanting him deep inside her? She could feel the melting heat of desire and the betraying prickle of her breasts as she tried to stop her body from pushing so insistently against his. Her breathing was shallow as it mingled with the warmth of his and she felt the moist flicker of his tongue, which promised so much pleasure. Oh, why was it Dimitri and only Dimitri who could ever make her feel this way? she thought despairingly.

Fleetingly, she wondered if Chico would do anything to stop what was happening—but what could he do, even if he was that kind of man? How could he tell Dimitri to back off when they were about to commit a crime? That this was nothing but a sham marriage, so that Chico could get his work permit.

She felt the bouquet slide from her nerveless fingers to the ground and she was afraid she might do the same when, suddenly, Dimitri terminated the kiss. His shadowed features tensed as he drew away from her—but not before his eyes had glittered out a warning and

Erin knew exactly what that warning meant. She had worked for him for years. She knew how his mind worked—at least, some of the time—and the message in their icy blue depths was as clear as day. *Leave this to me,* they said, and something inside her rebelled.

Did he really think he could waltz back into her life and start taking over, after all the grief he'd given her in the past? Because Dimitri was a man who *took,* she reminded herself grimly. Who took and took and never gave anything back. And he wasn't going to take anything else from her. Not any more. There were good reasons why he was no longer in her life—and even better ones why it should stay that way.

'How *dare* you?' she spat out, her voice shaking. 'What the hell do you think you're playing at?'

'You know exactly what I'm *playing* at, Erin.'

'You can't do this,' she said, meeting his gaze with a rebellious tilt of her chin. 'You can't.'

'No?' His pale eyes glittered in response. 'Just watch me.'

'Would someone mind explaining exactly what is going on?' asked the registrar, her polite tone not quite hiding her growing irritation. 'We have a number of weddings following yours and this unexpected interruption is—'

'There isn't going to be any wedding,' said Dimitri softly. 'Is there, Erin?'

They had all turned to look at her. Chico. The two witnesses. The registrar. But the only face Erin could see was Dimitri's and the icy challenge in his eyes. And suddenly it wasn't so easy to be rebellious. Suddenly, her certainties began to crumble as she recognised the glint of danger in the Russian's eyes.

She opened her mouth—so dry that it felt like parchment—before shutting it again with a snap. She looked at the faint frown on Chico's brow. Was he perceptive enough to know that if he dared confront Dimitri, he risked everything— that it would be like a centipede preparing to do battle with a lion? Or had the Russian effectively humiliated him by kissing his bride-to-be in full view of everyone, thus silencing any objections for ever?

But none of this mattered. Not really. Only Leo mattered and she didn't dare put his livelihood at risk. A mother being dragged in front of the courts for participating in a sham marriage could not really be deemed a fit mother. Imagine the shame and the terror and the very real threat of a fine—or even jail. Her mouth set into a determined line, because nothing like that was ever going to impact on her beloved son. Wasn't she only doing this to guarantee him a secure future and the feeling of safety which had always eluded her?

'I'm afraid it does look as if we might have to postpone the wedding,' she said, as apologetically as she could—though nothing in her vocabulary seemed a suitable response for such a bizarre situation. What could she say? She looked around nervously, like a stage compère facing a hostile audience. 'Dimitri is—'

'The only man she really wants—as her public capitulation has just proved,' said the Russian with cool arrogance and an even more arrogant smile, which only emphasised the rage in his eyes. 'Isn't that right, Erin?'

And now she saw something more than danger in his eyes. She saw the dark flicker of knowledge and Erin's heart twisted with pain. He *did* know! He *must* know. Had he somehow found out about Leo?

Her instinct was to get away from him and she wondered what would happen if she just picked up the skirts of her long dress and ran as fast as her feet could take her. The anonymous grey of the autumnal London day would swallow her up, leaving Dimitri far behind. She could take her wedding dress back to the same thrift shop from which she'd bought it. She could pick up Leo from school herself and tell him that Mummy wasn't going away on holiday after all and that they wouldn't be moving to a big house in the country.

If she ran away from him, she could cope—somehow. True, none of her immediate problems would have been solved, but she felt as if she could deal with anything as long as it wasn't beneath the Russian's unforgiving scrutiny and the fear of what he might or might not know.

But he had placed his hand at the small of her back—a light but proprietorial gesture which somehow managed to send out conflicting reactions of desire and dread. And she knew she wouldn't be running anywhere, any time soon.

'I'm sure this kind of thing happens all the time,' he said smoothly. 'The bride getting cold feet when she realises she's making a big mistake.'

The registrar put her pen down. 'Perhaps you would all like to leave the building,' she said quietly, 'and sort out your problems somewhere else?'

'My sentiments entirely. Do you happen to have

a room we could use to talk in private?' questioned Dimitri in a pleasant tone which didn't quite conceal the steely note of determination. And then he smiled and it was like the moon appearing from behind a dark cloud. 'Please?'

The registrar looked up at him, her disapproving expression melting away beneath the sensual impact of that unexpected smile.

'There is somewhere you can use,' she said grudgingly. 'But please don't be long.'

'Oh, we won't be long. It won't take long for me to say what I need to say,' said Dimitri softly, his hand still at the small of Erin's back. 'That I can promise you.'

'Come with me, then.'

They all followed the registrar out into the corridor and the two witnesses who'd been plucked from the street shrugged their shoulders and headed for the exit, probably to the nearest pub. Erin saw the shell-shocked expression on Chico's face as Dimitri ushered her past and her feelings of powerlessness only increased.

The registrar was opening the door to a featureless-looking room, but now that some of the initial shock was leaving her system Erin started to recover some of her equilibrium. *Remember why you were doing this,* she reminded herself fiercely. *There were good, solid reasons why you did what you did.*

And out there stood a confused man who had never been anything but a good friend to her.

Pulling away from Dimitri, she glared at him. 'I have to go and talk to Chico. I have to explain what is happening,' she said, even though she wasn't entirely sure herself. 'Wait here for me.'

But he caught hold of her wrist, his fingers vice-like against the frantic hammering of her pulse. 'Okay, speak to him if you must—but make it brief. And just make sure you come back, Erin,' he said, his voice cold. 'Because if you try to run away I will find you. Be in no doubt about that.'

She pulled away from him and went to find Chico, trying to explain why there wasn't going to be a wedding, her heart twisting with distress as she saw his face crumple. But by the time she returned to the featureless room where Dimitri was waiting, her distress had turned into anger and she was shaking with rage as she shut the door behind her. 'You had no right to do that!' she flared.

'I had every right,' he said. 'And you know it. And what is more—you didn't fight me very hard, did you? If you don't want a man near you, then you shouldn't kiss him as if you want him to do it to you right then and there.'

'You bastard.'

'Is that what I am, Erin?'

'You know you are!'

'Shouldn't you think very carefully about applying that *particular* word as an insult?'

His loaded words precipitated something—it must have been shock—for why else would her teeth have started chattering so violently? She made one last attempt at rebellion. *He has no real hold over you,* she told herself fiercely. *He's not your guardian or your keeper, or your boss.*

'I'm going now,' she said, meeting his eyes with a defiant stare. 'I want to go home.'

He laughed very softly and the sound filled her with dread.

'Please don't be delusional,' he said. 'We both know you aren't going anywhere—at least not until you and I have had a little talk. So sit down.'

Part of her wanted to object to the masterful way he sat her down on a nearby chair, but in truth she was grateful because her knees felt as if they might give way at any minute. But any feeling of gratitude was soon forgotten when she looked into the determined set of his face. She'd forgotten just how ruthless he could be. How he moved people around as if they were pawns on his own personal chessboard. As his secretary she'd been granted the rare gift of immunity to his whims, because once he had liked her and respected her.

Once.

Sitting huddled in her too-big wedding dress, she stared up at him. 'Now what?'

'Now you tell me all about your Brazilian lover,' he drawled. 'Is he hot between the sheets?'

'He isn't…' She hesitated, wondering how much he already knew. 'Chico isn't my lover—as I suspect you may have worked out for yourself, since he's gay.'

His mouth twisted. 'So it isn't a love match?'

'Hardly.'

'You're marrying a gay man,' he said slowly. 'Who I suspect is paying you for the privilege. Maybe he needs a visa, or a work permit.' His icy eyes glittered. 'Am I right, Erin?'

Did her face give her away? Did guilt wrap itself around her features so that he was able to give the smug smile of someone who'd just had his hunch confirmed?

'And that—as we both know—is against the law,' he continued softly.

Shaking herself out of her stupor, she glared at him, telling herself that attack was the best form of defence. 'Is that why you turned up out of the blue today, to point out the finer points of the law?' She willed herself not to show fear even though inside her heart was pumping like a piston. *Brazen it out,* she told herself. *Just brazen it out.* 'Is that what this is all about, Dimitri—are you about to report me to the authorities?'

Suddenly, his face changed and Erin knew that when he spoke his voice would be different, too. It would be steely and matter-of-fact instead of mocking and casual. He was bored with playing games and was about to cut to the chase. She knew him much too well.

'But you already know the answer to that question, Erin. You've known since the moment you turned round and saw me. You just haven't had the guts to come out and admit it.' In the featureless room with the blinds drawn down to block out the outside world, his eyes glittered like shards of blue ice. 'Or maybe you were intending to keep my son hidden from me for ever—was that your plan?'

CHAPTER TWO

DIMITRI SAW ALL the colour drain from Erin's face and felt a beat of something which felt very close to satisfaction. He watched as she leaned her head back against the wall—as if the weight of her head were too much for that slender neck to support—and looked at him warily, her green eyes slitted. He didn't know what had hurt the most. No, not hurt. He didn't do hurt. Mentally, he corrected himself. What had *angered* him most. The fact that she hadn't told him, or the fact that she had lied to him, when once he would have counted Erin Turner as about the only truly honest person he'd ever known. She was still trying to lie—he could see it in the sudden whitening of her face and the way she was nervously licking her lips. He found himself thinking that she would make a useless poker player.

'Your son?' she said, as if it were a word she'd never heard before.

Her disingenuous question sealed his rage and Dimitri tensed, not daring to respond until he had his emotions under control, because not once in all his turbulent thirty-six years could he ever recall feeling such anger. Not even towards his cheating mother or crooked father. Instinct made him want to lash out at her. To haul her towards him and hurl his accusations straight into her lying face. To ask why *she*—of all people—would have betrayed him. But he had been successful for long enough to know that it was far more effective to hide the edge of anger beneath the velvet cloak of smoothness, even if Erin was one of the few people who would know how angry he really was.

'Oh, come on, Erin,' he said silkily. 'Please don't try to assume the role of innocent, because it insults my intelligence. You should have had an answer to this question by now because you must have been expecting that I would turn up and ask it at some point. Or did you really think I would never find out? Maybe not this year, or even next—but surely you must have anticipated that one day I would be confronting you like this to ask you about your son. *My* son.'

He thought she looked like a textbook study of guilt. She was looking from side to side, like an animal which had been cornered, and it was difficult for Dimitri to reconcile himself with this new version of her. The white-faced woman in the ill-fitting wedding gown was nothing like the Erin he'd known. The smart and straightforward woman who had worked by his side for years, ever since she'd left secretarial college. Who, unlike every other woman on the planet, had never flirted with him and had thus earned his grudging respect. She was the person who'd been given unprecedented access to all areas of his life and affairs. The one person he had trusted above all others. And yes, sleeping with her that one time had been a mistake. Definitely. It had quickly become apparent that things could never

be the same between them afterwards—but even
so how dared she keep the consequences of that
night from him for all these years?

How dared she?

'You aren't going to deny it, are you, Erin?' he
continued mockingly. 'Because you can't.'

Her lips opened and she shivered and, pow-
ered by an instinct he wasn't sure he recognised, Dimitri removed his jacket and draped
it around her narrow shoulders. The suit's grey
jacket swamped her and made her complexion
look even more waxy than it had been before
and his mouth hardened. Was she opening those
green eyes as wide as a kitten and thinking he
would take pity on her? Because if that was the
case—she was wrong.

Very wrong.

There was a tap on the door and a woman
poked her head in, before mouthing *sorry* apologetically and withdrawing again.

'Let's get out of here,' he said coldly.

He half lifted her out of the chair and ushered

her outside, where a cold blast of autumnal air cut right through her and Erin was aware of people turning to stare as if the tall, molten-haired man were abducting the shivering bride. Instantly, a sleek black limousine purred to a halt in front of them and Dimitri opened up the door and bundled her inside. Sliding onto the seat beside her, he gave a peremptory tap on the window and the car began to move away.

'Where are we going?' she questioned, looking around her in alarm. 'Where are you taking me?'

'Cut the dramatics,' he snapped. 'We need to have a conversation, so it's your place or mine. Up to you.'

His words were greeted with the expression of someone who had just been offered a choice of two poisons to drink, for she bit her bottom lip, bringing a little colour to its plump fullness. And suddenly Dimitri found himself remembering the way he'd kissed her in the register office—a kiss born out of rage and a desire to take control. A kiss intended to show young Chico exactly who was boss—as if any such demonstration were really needed. But it hadn't worked out quite as he'd intended, had it? He hadn't meant it to kick-start his libido, but it had. And despite his rage and disbelief, it was as much as he could do not to kiss her again. To pull her into his arms and feel that ripe, young body close to his, opening up like a flower. He'd forgotten just how instantly she went up in flames the moment he touched her. How her fairly commonplace exterior hid a powerful sexuality, which was both unexpected and surprising.

He could see her swallowing—the movement rippling down that swanlike neck of hers. And he could hear the note of anxiety which had entered her voice.

'Why can't we just have the conversation here?'

'I think you know the answer to that, Erin. Apart from wanting complete privacy—and my driver speaks perfect English as well as Russian—I don't think I trust myself to be in such a confined space with you when we are discussing something which I'm still having difficulty getting my head round.' His voice lowered into a harsh rasp. 'Discovering that I have a son and that you have kept him hidden from me for all these years is bad enough and I might be tempted into doing something which I might later regret. So you'd better make up your mind about where we're going, or I'll be forced to make the decision for you.'

Erin pulled the jacket closer around her shoulders—grateful for the warmth but wishing that the expensive cloth were not permeated with Dimitri's distinctive scent. She was trapped—in every which way. She didn't want to take him to the home she shared with Leo and her sister, Tara. Not because she was ashamed of the rather humble dwelling. No, the truth was more worrying than that. She was terrified of him seeing Leo. Afraid he might just take command and grab the child—stealing him away from her and thinking he was perfectly entitled to. Because mightn't she attempt something similar if the situation were reversed? If she'd discovered that someone had kept her flesh and blood hidden from her like some kind of guilty secret for all these years?

A feeling of despair washed over her as she contemplated what lay ahead, knowing that further lies and evasion were pointless. And besides, hadn't this been a long time coming? How many times over the years had she picked up the telephone to tell him about the blue-eyed little boy who was his spitting image? Hadn't her heart sometimes burned with the pain of denying her boy access to his father? Until she had forced herself to remember the truth about the man and his appalling lifestyle.

She remembered the hours he'd spent in nightclubs and bars and casinos, gambling away millions of rubles as if they were nothing but loose change, in a vodka- or whisky-induced haze. She remembered all the women who had passed through his bed—the ones with the tiny dresses and tottering heels who exuded a dangerous kind of glamour, along with the occasional flash of their knickers. She certainly didn't want her son growing up to think those kind of women were the norm. Who was to say that the seedy world Dimitri inhabited wouldn't corrupt her golden-haired boy and introduce him to some unspeakable future?

She remembered his coldness towards her the morning after she'd slept with him—his shocked face when he'd opened his eyes and seen who was lying beside him. With her brown hair and narrow build she must have seemed like a different species from the blowsy women he usually bedded. No wonder he hadn't been able to wait to get away from her.

'We'd better go to your place, I suppose,' she said, her voice filled with resignation.

His mouth hardened as he rapped on the window and spoke to the driver in his native tongue, and the car took a left, travelling towards the dockland area of the city.

Erin waited for his interrogation to begin, but

when Dimitri took a phone call and began what was clearly a business conversation in his native Russian, she was momentarily perplexed. Until she remembered that his ability to switch on and off was legendary. And he was manipulative—that was one of the reasons he was so frighteningly successful. Right now, he would have realised that by leaving her to stew he would only increase her feelings of insecurity and put him in an even stronger position. His clever mind would be carefully stockpiling a series of questions, but he would ask them only in his time, and on his terms.

And really, there was only one question which she was going to have difficulty answering...

The car took them to his skyscraper apartment overlooking the river and Erin was filled with a horrible feeling of déjà vu as they walked into the magnificent marbled foyer, with its forest of tall, potted palms—behind which sat one of the burly porters who were all ju-jitsu trained. Sometimes she used to come here to take dictation if her boss was getting ready to go abroad, and it was a place she had always liked—a coldly magnificent apartment which was worlds away from her own rented home. She'd liked the river view and the fact that you could push a button and the blinds would float down, or another button would send music drifting out from one of the many speakers. She'd liked pretty much everything about it until the night when she'd overstepped the mark. When she'd offered him comfort during the one time she'd seen Dimitri looking vulnerable.

And he'd responded by taking her virginity on his vast dining-room table, tearing off her panties like a man possessed and making that almost *feral* moan as he drove deep inside her.

She could see the porter looking her up and down as she stepped out of the revolving door in her badly fitting white dress, with Dimitri's jacket hanging around her shoulders. Briefly, she felt like some sort of crazy woman, especially when he propelled her into the waiting elevator at great speed.

'Hurry up,' he said as he pressed the button for the penthouse elevator. 'I don't want my reputation being trashed by being seen with a woman in a second-hand wedding dress.'

'I didn't think it was possible for your reputation to sink any lower!'

Pale eyes swept over her. 'You might be surprised how out of touch you are,' he said mockingly.

'I doubt it,' she spat back.

But as the elevator gathered speed Erin knew she had to forget the past and concentrate on the present. She had to think about the situation as it *was*, not what it used to be. If only she hadn't allowed her feelings for him to ruin everything. If only she hadn't started entertaining romantic fantasies about him—when she knew better than anyone that grand passion brought with it nothing but disillusionment.

She bunched up the material of her white dress as he unlocked his apartment and stood aside to let her pass, and she couldn't work out whether to be happy or sad when she noticed that very little had changed. The vast, wooden-floored entrance hall still provided the perfect backdrop for all the Russian artefacts which were everywhere. The Fabergé eggs he collected were displayed in a casual grouping, which only seemed to emphasise their priceless beauty. There was one in particular which she used to love—a perfect golden sphere studded with emeralds and rubies, which seemed to mock her now as it sparkled in the autumn sunlight.

'Come with me,' he said, as if he didn't trust her to be out of his sight for a second.

He walked into the main reception—a room dominated by a panoramic view over the river and the glittering skyscrapers which housed much of the city's wealth. Yet it was the room itself which drew the eye as much as the view. He had always kept bonsai trees—exquisite miniature trees which experts came in weekly to tend. Sitting on a polished table was a Japanese Acer—its tiny leaves the bright red colour of a sunset.

Erin stared at it with the delight of someone en-
countering an old friend. How she had always
loved that little tree.

But as she glanced up from the vibrant leaves
she saw in Dimitri's eyes the unmistakable flicker
of fury.

'So. Start explaining,' he bit out.

Her knees had suddenly gone wobbly and she
sat down on one of the leather sofas, even though
he hadn't asked her to—terrified of appearing
weak when she knew it was vital to stay strong.
She looked up into his face and tried to keep her
voice steady. 'I don't think it needs very much
of an explanation, do you? You are as aware of
the facts as I am. We spent that night together...'

Her words trailed off because it still felt faintly
unbelievable that she'd ended up in his bed, when
he could have had any woman on the planet. And
yes, she'd found him attractive—in the way that
you sometimes looked at the ocean and were ren-
dered speechless by its power and beauty. Erin
certainly hadn't been immune to the carved sym-

metry of Dimitri's proud Russian features, or the hair which gleamed like dark gold. There probably wasn't a woman alive who wouldn't have looked twice at his powerful body or admired his clever mind or the way a rare flash of humour could sometimes lighten his cold face. But she had never let her admiration show, because that was unprofessional—and she was pragmatic enough to know that she was the kind of woman he would never find attractive, even if she hadn't been his secretary.

She had worked for him for years. He'd plucked her from a lowly job within his organisation—mainly, she suspected, because she didn't go into instant meltdown whenever he came into the room. She had trained herself not to be affected by his sex appeal and a charisma undimmed by his haughty arrogance. She'd tried to treat him as she would treat anyone else, with dignity and respect. She had been calm and capable in the face of any storm—he'd told her that often enough. Soon he'd started giving her more and more responsibility until gradually the job had begun to take over her life, so that she'd had little left of her own. Maybe it was always that way when you worked for a powerful oligarch, with fingers in so many pies that he could have done with an extra pair of hands. She'd lost count of the times when she'd had to take a call from him during a dinner date, or miss the second half of a film because Dimitri had been flying in from Russia and needed her.

And she'd liked that feeling of being needed, hadn't she? She'd liked the fact that such a powerful man used to listen to *her*—plain, ordinary Erin Turner. Maybe her ego was bigger than she'd given it credit for. Maybe it was that same ego which was responsible for allowing her feelings to slip from the consummate professional to being a woman with a stupid crush, despite her increasing awareness of the murkier side of her boss's life. She began to nurture feelings about him which were unaffected by his gambling and clubbing and drinking and women. And those feelings began to grow.

She used to watch in mild horror from the sidelines as he played the part of the wild oligarch as if it were going out of fashion—as if he'd needed to prove something to the world, and to himself. There had been luxury yachts and private jets stopping off at Mediterranean fleshpots and Caribbean islands—always with some supermodel hanging on to his arm like a limpet. He'd mixed with empty-eyed men with faces even harder than his own. His hangovers had been legendary. He'd been…reckless—embracing life in the fast lane with a hunger and a speed which had seemed to be getting more and more out of control. Even his trusted bodyguard, Loukas Sarantos, had ended up resigning in frustration as Erin had looked on in despair. She remembered ringing up Loukas in desperation after he'd left—and the terrible bust-up in Paris which had followed.

Had it been her growing feelings for Dimitri which had made her start watching out for him, above and beyond the call of duty? Why she'd gone round to his apartment one dark and rainy night, a stack of papers beneath her arm—worried because he hadn't been answering his phone and she'd been imagining the worst?

She remembered that her hand had been shaking as she'd rung the doorbell and had started shaking even more when he'd answered the door wearing nothing but a tiny towel, his bronzed body still damp and gleaming from the shower. Erin had been so relieved to see him that she'd been struck dumb, until it had dawned on her that he was almost naked. And that his face was dark and unsmiling.

'Yes?' he said impatiently. 'What is it, Erin?'

Even now she could remember the hard pounding of her heart. 'I've…er…I've brought some papers for you to sign.'

He frowned as he began to walk towards the dining room and made an impatient indication that she follow him. 'Couldn't they have waited until the morning?'

Faced with the sight of her powerful and very sexy boss wearing nothing but a tiny towel was playing havoc with her breathing, but Erin remembered looking at him very steadily as she put the papers down on the table.

'Actually, I was worried about you.'

'And what precisely were you worried about?'

'You haven't been answering your phone.'

'So?'

Painfully aware of his proximity and the heat of his body, Erin was struck dumb. She'd planned to say something on the lines of wishing he wouldn't keep such dangerous company, but the only thing she could think of right then was the danger of being alone with him like this.

She wondered if something in her expression gave away the desire which was shooting through her. Or whether it was the way she nervously licked her lips which made his body tense like that. His eyes seemed drawn to the involuntary movement of her tongue and then he nodded, like someone doing a complicated mathematical puzzle and coming up with a totally unexpected answer.

'Oh, I see,' he said, his lips curving into a predatory smile. 'And there was me thinking you were the one woman who was immune to my charms, Erin.'

She didn't even get a chance to object to his arrogance because without warning he gave a low laugh and pulled her against him—his lips covering hers in a hard kiss, as if he was trying out a new kind of sport. And Erin dissolved because she'd never been kissed like that before. Never. Within seconds of that kiss, she was so aroused that she barely noticed that the towel had slipped from his hips. It was only when her hand slipped down his back to encounter the rocky globe of a bare buttock that her eyes snapped open as she stared into his.

'Shocked?' he drawled.

'N-no.'

'I think you want me,' he said unevenly as he

began to unbutton her jacket. 'Do you want me, *zvezda moya*?'

Did the sun rise every morning?

Of *course* she wanted him.

Erin gasped with hunger and delight as he pulled the navy jacket impatiently from her shoulders and unclipped the matching pencil skirt so that it slid to the ground.

She thought he might carry her into the bedroom, the way he'd done so often in her wilder fantasies. But instead he laid her out on the dining-room table—like some kind of sacrificial offering—and things happened very quickly after that. He started tearing hungrily at her underwear and she was shocked by how much she *liked* that, writhing her hips in silent hunger as she urged him on. She had vague memories of him putting on a condom and making some remark about how aroused she was making him feel. And then he thrust deep inside her and it wasn't a dream, or a fantasy—it was really happening.

She had been a virgin, but he didn't mention

it—and neither did she. She wasn't even sure he'd noticed. And it hadn't hurt the way people warned you it might—maybe because she wanted him so much. All she knew was that she'd never seen Dimitri looking quite so out of control. As if the universe could have exploded around them and he wouldn't have paid it a blind bit of attention.

She remembered that first urgent thrust—as if he'd wanted to lose something of himself deep inside her. And hadn't she felt exactly the same? As if her whole life had been spent in preparation for that moment. She remembered the way she'd shuddered with pleasure, orgasming not once, but twice, in rapid succession. And he had laughed—softly and triumphantly—running his fingertip over her trembling lips and telling her that she handled better than any of his cars.

'Yes, we spent the night together,' he said impatiently, completing her sentence, and Erin blinked as Dimitri's voice shattered her erotic memories. She came back to the present with a start—to the

cheap wedding dress and the unforgiving coldness of his face as he paced around his vast apartment.

'We had a night of sex which should never have
happened,' he continued harshly. 'I thought we
both decided that. That it had been a mistake.'

Erin nodded. That was what he had said the
morning after, and she'd felt there had been no
choice but to agree. What else could she have
done—clung to his naked body and begged him
to stay with her and do it to her all over again?
Told him that she wanted to care for him and save
him, and keep him safe from the awful world he
inhabited? She remembered the bedcovers falling away from her breasts and the sombre look
which had come over his face. The way he'd suddenly got out of bed, as if he hadn't been able to
wait to get away from her. His final words had
killed off any hopes she might have had for a repeat. 'I'm not the kind of man you need, Erin,'
he'd said abruptly. 'Go and find yourself some-

one nice and kind. Someone who will treat you the way you should be treated.'

After that, dignity had seemed the only way forward, especially when he'd left the country the next day and kept communication brief and un-emotional during the weeks which had followed.

'And we used a condom,' he said, his brow fur-rowing and his lips flattening into a scowl. 'I al-ways do.'

His words seemed intended to remind her that she was just one of many and Erin looked at him, her clasped hands feeling sticky as she buried them within the folds of her wedding dress. 'I know we did,' she said.

'I never wanted a child,' he added bitterly.

She knew that, too. He'd made no secret of his thoughts about marriage and childhood. That marriage was an expensive waste of time and some people were never cut out for parenthood. Was that one of the reasons why she'd balked at telling him about her pregnancy—terrified he would try to prevent her from having his baby?

She remembered going round to his apartment, sick with dread at the thought of blurting out her momentous news—and what she had found there had made her turn around and never go back…

But his condemnatory words were bringing something to life inside her and that something was a mother's protective instinct. She thought of Leo's innocent face—all flushed and warm after his evening bath—and a feeling of strength washed over her. 'Then pretend you don't have a child,' she said fiercely. 'Pretend that nothing has changed, because I have no intention of forcing something on you which you don't want. You can walk away and forget you ever found out. Leave me with our son and don't let it trouble your conscience. Leo and I can manage perfectly well on our own.'

Erin saw something which almost looked like *pleasure* flickering in his icy eyes and she remembered that dissent was something he was used to dealing with. Something he seemed almost to *enjoy*. Because dissent implied battle and Dimitri Makarov always won the battles he fought.

'You can manage perfectly well?' he questioned softly.

'Yes,' she said, aware on some level that she was walking into a trap, but not knowing exactly where that trap lay.

'So how come I found you standing in a cheap wedding dress, about to break the law?'

She licked her lips but didn't answer.

'Why, Erin?'

'I had my reasons.'

'And I want to hear them.'

She hesitated, knowing she could procrastinate no longer. 'Leo and I live with my sister. She owns a café in Bow.'

'I know that.'

Had her face registered her shock and surprise? 'How could you possibly know that?'

'I had some of my people investigate you.'

'You had *what*? Why?' She could hear her

voice beginning to tremble. 'Why would you do something like that?'

'Because of the child, of course.' His pale eyes narrowed into icy shards. 'Why else?'

'How did you find out about Leo?'

'The means are irrelevant,' he snapped. 'Just accept that I did. Now, where were we?'

Her heart sinking, she stared at him, knowing that she was trapped. 'Leo goes to a local school and he's doing very well, but...'

He bit out the words like bullets. 'But what?'

She tried to keep the fear from her voice. The fear that she wasn't doing the best for the golden child who had inherited so many of his father's qualities.

'He's good at sport and there just aren't the facilities where we live. The nearest park is a good bus ride away and Tara and I are often too busy working in the café to take him. You remember Tara? She's my sister.'

'I remember,' he said tightly.

She drew in a deep breath, hoping to see some

softening or understanding on the granite features, but there was none. And suddenly she wanted him to understand that there were reasons why she'd agreed to the marriage today. Good reasons. 'Chico comes from a rich family in Brazil and wants to stay in England. He offered me a large sum of money to marry him, so that he could get a work permit. I was planning on using the money to resettle. To…to take Leo to the countryside and live somewhere with a garden. Somewhere he could kick a ball around and get plenty of fresh air and exercise. I…I want him to have that kind of life.'

Still his face showed no sign of reaction as he walked over to the large fireplace and pressed a bell recessed into the wall beside it. Moments later, a young woman appeared—a beautiful, cool blonde. Of course she was blonde. Every woman in the Russian's life, bar Erin, was fair—sporting every shade in the spectrum from spun gold to moonbeam pale, because Dimitri needed blondes in the same way other men needed to breathe.

Her flaxen hair was cut into a soft bob and her high cheekbones marked her out as Slavic, so it came as no surprise when Dimitri spoke to her in Russian. She glanced briefly over at Erin and nodded, before turning on her high-heeled shoes and leaving the room again.

Still Dimitri said nothing and in a way his silence was far more intimidating than if he'd continued to subject her to a barrage of angry questions. Would she ever be able to convince him that she'd tried to act in everyone's best interests?

Erin was surprised when the blonde returned a few minutes later, carrying a pair of jeans and a cashmere sweater over her arm. She walked across the room and, placing them on the table in front of her, she smiled.

'I think they will fit you,' she said, her cut-glass English accent seeming to contradict the fluent Russian she'd used moments before. 'But I have a belt you can use if the jeans are too big.'

'*Spasiba*, Sofia,' growled Dimitri, watching

as the blonde left the room with that same confident wiggle.

Erin stared at the clothes. 'What are these for?'

'What do they look like they're for? Sofia is lending you some of her own clothes,' he said. 'Put them on. I'm taking you home and I want as few people as possible seeing you. A woman leaving my apartment wearing a wedding dress would be bound to get the press excited, and I make a point of steering clear of the newspapers these days.'

Erin narrowed her eyes. Was that why he hadn't featured in any of his famous post-nightclub shots with a half-clothed woman in tow recently? Was he getting better at hiding his seedy lifestyle?

She felt like refusing his autocratic demand to wear someone else's clothes but she was cold now and she was starting to shiver. Maybe it was reaction. 'Okay, I'll put the jeans on,' she said, from between chattering teeth. 'But I don't need you to take me home afterwards. I'm perfectly capable of catching the bus.'

'I don't think you quite understand the situation, Erin,' he said coldly. 'Unless you are trying to be coy, thinking I might take pity on you and let you go. Because that's not going to happen. So let me spell it out for you, so that you get the message loud and clear.' His eyes glittered like early-morning sun on ice. 'I am taking you home so that I can meet my son.'

CHAPTER THREE

'YOU CAN'T,' SAID Erin fervently as the limousine gathered speed, and she turned to look at Dimitri, who was sitting like some granite-faced sentry in the back seat beside her. Sofia's designer jeans were indeed too big but the baby-blue sweater hugged her nicely and now she was warmer she felt more in control. She made one last attempt to appeal to the Russian's better nature, even if deep in her heart she knew he didn't have one. 'You can't just turn up out of the blue and introduce yourself to a six-year-old boy and tell him you're his long-lost father.'

'Just watch me,' he said grimly.

Erin heard the harsh note in his voice and was reminded of his fierce reputation. Not that he had minded. He always maintained that a fierce reputation kept fools at a distance and for a long time she had been flattered by that statement and its implication. Because *she* had been one of the few people he'd allowed to get close to him—and hadn't that made her think she meant more to him than she actually did? Oh, the foolish longings of a rich man's secretary!

'Think about it, Dimitri,' she said quietly.

'What do you think I've been doing?' he demanded. 'I've done nothing but think about it since I was first shown a photograph of the boy.'

'And when was that?'

'Seven days ago,' he snapped.

She nodded, determined not to let him sweep her aside with the force of his anger, knowing she had to fight her little boy's corner here. For his sake. For all their sakes. 'Leo doesn't know you—'

'And whose fault is that?'

A wave of remorse washed over her and suddenly her decision didn't seem quite so clear-cut. Because Dimitri *did* seem different. The clear-eyed man in the pristine suit was light years away from the stubble-jawed and hungover man who used to arrive at the office demanding strong coffee. 'Mine,' she admitted. 'But I did it with the best intentions.'

'I don't care about your intentions, Erin,' he said, his voice dipping. 'I just care about what is mine. And this child is my flesh and blood, too, not just yours.'

His unashamed possessiveness sent a ripple of alarm through her and Erin recognised that once a piece of information was out there, you couldn't get it back. And you couldn't control the outcome, either. Dimitri was here and—judging from the grim expression on his face—he was here to stay.

'If you really care about him,' she said, 'then you must take it slowly. Imagine how it would feel if you suddenly exploded into his life without warning.'

'You should have considered that before, shouldn't you?'

The car drew up in front of a set of red traffic lights and a man on a bike raced past them, using the inside lane. Erin listened to the blare of horns which greeted the cyclist's action as she thought how best to get Dimitri to see sense. He liked facts, didn't he? Hard, cold facts. *So present them to him.*

She sucked in a deep breath. 'You always used to say you had no desire to be a father.'

'Given the choice,' came his flat response. 'Which I haven't been.'

'And what if that's still true? You might meet him and wish you never had. It might reinforce all the worst things you ever thought about fatherhood. And if that were the case, wouldn't it be hard for you to walk away and even harder for him to pretend that the meeting had never happened?'

Dimitri's lips tightened as her words struck an unwanted chord, thinking how well she knew him—better perhaps than anyone else. What if he met the child, but could not meet the boy's expectations? What if the boy wanted love from him—real love—and commitment? Could he take that risk, knowing that he could provide none of those things?

'What are you suggesting?' he demanded.

She met his gaze without flinching. 'I don't know you any more. I have to be sure that you're no longer the man you used to be. You have to convince me that you've changed. I don't want Leo mixing with gamblers or heavy drinkers, or witnessing a stream of women parading their bodies in front of him.'

His mouth twisted. 'You mean you want to vet me?'

'Can you blame me?' she retorted. 'But we also need to discuss what to say to him. If you're going to meet Leo after all this time, we need to present a united front.'

Dimitri felt his body tense as she stated her demands. As if what *she* wanted was the only thing which mattered. There was no sense of remorse that she'd kept this information from him for so long, was there? Not a flicker of it...

Anger bubbled up inside him and suddenly he felt the need to lash out. Without thinking, he caught hold of her arms—thinking how slim they felt beneath the borrowed sweater. She jerked her head back in surprise so that the light caught the cheap, fake pearls which were woven into her hair. Her lips were parted, her green eyes were dark and, although her face was wary, he realised that she still wanted him. That in the midst of everything, there was desire. Of course there was. No female remained immune to him for long. He could feel sexual hunger pulsating in the air around them as his gaze flickered to the twin thrust of her nipples pinpointing against the soft wool of the sweater. He thought how easy it would be to burrow his hands beneath. To caress those hard little nubs with the skill which could sometimes make a woman come, just by doing that. For a nanosecond he was tempted beyond measure, his fingers longing to creep over those tiny mounds and play with them.

Until he remembered that this was the woman who had deliberately concealed his son from him. Who had written him out of her life as if he no longer existed. How could he possibly desire a woman like that? Abruptly, he dropped his hands, wondering if she was aware that disappointment was written all over her face as he did so. A flicker of triumph coursed through him as she bit her lip and he took a moment to enjoy her obvious frustration.

'So what were you planning to do after your wedding?' he questioned. 'Were you coming back here to the café with your new husband to parade your shiny new ring for all to see?'

'No. We'd…we'd planned to spend a long weekend at a hotel in the country. Chico took my suitcase down there yesterday.'

'For your *honeymoon*?' he scorned.

'I suppose you could call it that. It was intended

to make our marriage seem more authentic to the authorities, that was all.'

'So Leo knows about the wedding?'

There was silence for a moment. 'Of course he does,' she said. 'He likes Chico. We were… We were all going to live together in a lovely house in the country.'

'A fake marriage to a gay man—with separate rooms, I presume?' he said. 'How the hell was that supposed to work?'

'We would have *made* it work,' she defended. 'I was thinking about Leo's future. About giving him the financial security I could never guarantee him!'

'What kind of example is that to set for a child?' he demanded bitterly, because he was discovering a nerve which was still raw, even after all these years. 'Basing your life on lies and deception?'

Nervously, she glanced out of the window. 'I don't want to talk about it any more. At least, not now,' she said, her voice growing strained. 'Because we're nearly there.'

He followed the direction of her gaze to the grey, treeless streets outside. 'And will my son be there?'

She flinched a little, as if it hurt to hear him use the possessive phrase. Well, *tough*, he thought grimly. She was going to have to get used to a lot more than that.

'No. He'll still be at school. He won't be back for a couple of hours.'

Dimitri flexed his fingers as he forced himself to think about practicalities, because he could see that she was right. He couldn't just burst in, unannounced—and although it went against his every instinct, he could see that the process should be gradual. Yet his discovery about the boy could not have come at a worse time, because he was due to travel to Jazratan tomorrow, for some delicate end-stage negotiations with the Sheikh of that oil-rich land. It was a deal which had been a long time in the making, and Saladin Al Mektala was not a man whose presence you could postpone. But Dimitri recognised suddenly that this discovery was more important than any deal—and the realisation surprised him almost as much as the unexpected twist of his heart when he thought of his unknown son. Because he was a man who put business above everything—who never allowed his personal life to intrude on his material ambitions.

He glanced at Erin, but she wasn't looking at him. Her head was bent and the fake pearls were glinting in her dark hair. He guessed he could start getting to know Leo when he returned from his desert trip, but he was reluctant to let her out of his sight. What if she disappeared while he was away, taking Leo with her? If she was determined for him not to meet his son, he wouldn't put it past her. He wouldn't put anything past her.

Unless… Restlessly, he tapped his finger against one taut thigh as he began to sift through all the options which lay open to him and the germ of an idea came to him. It wasn't perfect, but it was simple—if he could persuade her to accept it. His mouth hardened, knowing he would make her accept it, whether she liked it or not.

'So if the wedding is off and you were due to go away for the weekend, then Leo won't be expecting you home?' he said.

'N-no,' she answered uncertainly, as if sensing a trap.

'Then listen to me very carefully, Erin—because this is what you are going to do. You will go and pack yourself another bag.'

She stilled. 'What for?'

'Think about it. You said that you needed to get to know me and that we needed to present a united front when I meet Leo—so that's exactly what we're going to do. As it happens, I'm booked to go to Jazratan this weekend to stay at the royal palace—'

'Not with the horse-mad Sheikh?'

Her instant recall of his business dealings made him give a reluctant nod of satisfaction. 'That's the one.'

'You're not still trying to buy some of his oil wells?'

'Indeed I am. And I am this close…' he held up

his thumb and forefinger, with a distance of an inch between them '…to succeeding. Which is why the trip cannot be cancelled—and why you will be accompanying me.'

'Me?' Her voice was a squeak as her hands tightened into balled fists. 'Why on earth would I come with you to Jazratan?'

'Why not? It will provide us with the space we need. I'll have to run it past the Sheikh's advisors first, but I can foresee no problem. You were the best secretary I've ever had and you've worked on some of the negotiations with me in the past. I can say that I want you beside me if and when I sign the biggest deal of my life.'

She stared at him. 'Are you…*out of your mind*?'

Abruptly, his mood seemed to change. Gone was the element of negotiation and in its place was a steely determination she recognised only too well.

'No, I am not out of my mind,' he iced back. 'I am trying to work out a solution and I am fighting every instinct I possess not to go in there and tell that little boy the truth. To tell him that not only is his mother a liar, but that she has kept me completely out of the loop. I don't think the courts look very favourably on that kind of behaviour these days. A mother denying her child access to his father is seen as selfish, not noble— and gone are the days when a father has no rights. So are you going to accept my suggestion, Erin— or are you going to waste time by arguing with me, when we both know I always get what I want in the end?'

Yes, he did.

Always.

Erin tried to get her head around his words. *Accompany him to Jazratan, to stay in a desert palace?*

He couldn't force her...yet if she turned him down, her refusal to cooperate would surely impact on Leo. Her gaze strayed to his stony profile and she saw a nerve flickering at his temple— an indication he had reached the limit of his patience, a quality for which he had never been renowned. And she knew he was right. There was no point in fighting him. Because he *would* win.

'It seems I have no choice,' she said.

He smiled, but the smile didn't touch his eyes. 'That is possibly the first sensible thing you've said all day,' he said. 'So go and get your stuff together and explain to your sister that there's been a change of plan.' He pulled a card from his pocket and handed it to her. 'This is my private number. She can contact you via this should the need arise while we're away.'

Erin took the card from him as the limousine drew up at the end of her road and thoughts of escape overwhelmed her as she reached for the door handle. What if he turned up at the appointed time and she and Leo weren't there—he would have to leave for Jazratan without her, wouldn't he?

But almost as if he'd read her mind, he reached out and caught hold of her and Erin could feel her pulse rocketing as his fingers curled over her wrist.

'This is going to happen, make no mistake. So don't keep me waiting and don't even think about running away,' he said softly. 'You have precisely one hour and then my car will return for you. Do you understand?'

Erin was still shaking as she watched him drive away, taking a moment to compose herself as she pushed open the door of the Oranges & Lemons café, which her sister had named after a famous nursery rhyme about the church bells of London. It was a bright and cheerful place, decorated with framed paintings of the fruits done by local children, and usually Erin enjoyed that first explosion of colour whenever she walked in. But today all she could think about were a pair of icy eyes and the harsh words Dimitri had spoken to her.

Her sister, Tara, was polishing glasses behind the counter and she looked up in surprise when she saw her, blinking behind her owl-like glasses.

'Erin! What on earth are you doing here? You look terrible,' she added before lowering her voice, even though there were hardly any customers around. 'Did something happen? Did it...' She hesitated, her face twisting with a funny kind of expression. 'Did the wedding all go off as planned?'

'No,' said Erin flatly. 'It didn't.'

Tara stared. 'Whose clothes are you wearing?'

For a minute Erin didn't know what her sister was talking about and then looked down and realised she was wearing another woman's sweater and a pair of jeans which didn't fit her properly. 'It's a long story,' she said and then, stupidly, her voice began to wobble and for one awful moment she thought she was about to cry. She swallowed, because she wasn't going to do that. She mustn't do that. Staying calm needed to be her focus, not making stupid displays of unnecessary emotion. She drew a deep breath and tried to make her voice sound as bland as if she were announcing what was showing on TV that night. 'Dimitri Makarov turned up.'

Tara's face blanched. 'He actually *turned up*?'

'That's right. He—'

'For God's sake.' Tara put the glass down with a hand which was far from steady. 'Come round here and sit down. I'll make you a coffee.'

'I don't want any coffee.' But Erin walked behind the bar all the same and noticed that Tara was making her a cup anyway. She watched her grinding beans and driving steam into the small cup, and forced herself to take a sip of the espresso which was pushed firmly along the counter towards her.

'So, what happened?' asked Tara.

Briefly, Erin explained—though it sounded like the plot of an old film as she recounted how Dimitri had stormed in to halt the wedding, before taking her back to his place to lay down the law.

'He did that?' questioned Tara shakily.

'He did.' Erin's voice was grim. 'He wants to see Leo. He wants to get to know him.' And suddenly it wasn't quite so easy to stay focused. Suddenly, it was all too easy to see how problematic this was going to be. 'He's coming back in an hour and he wants me packed and ready.'

'Packed and ready for what?'

'You're not going to believe me if I tell you.'

'Try me.'

Erin wriggled shoulders which were stiff with tension. 'He's taking me to Jazratan. It's a country in the Middle East—one of the richest of the desert states, as it happens. He thinks we ought to get to know each other better before he's introduced to Leo.'

Tara frowned. 'And what's that supposed to mean?'

'I *don't know*.' Beads of sweat broke out on Erin's brow and she brushed them away with the back of her hand. She told herself she didn't have to do anything she didn't want to. But that was the trouble. With Dimitri it wasn't that simple—nothing ever was. Whenever she looked at him she started thinking about things which were forbidden. Things she was never going to have. Things she didn't even believe in. And she'd made that mistake once before. She'd thought she'd been in love when she'd woken up in his bed that morning and look where it had got her. His look of shock and horror had stripped away all her stupid delusions. Her *grand passion* had gone the way of all grand passions—it had burnt itself out before it had even had the chance to get started. It had reinforced everything she'd always known about letting your heart rule your head— and no way was she going to repeat that mistake. Her life hadn't been easy since she'd handed in her notice—but at least she hadn't had to live with the unbearable pain of heartbreak.

She pushed away her cup before looking up at her sister with bewildered eyes. 'The only thing I can't work out is how he found out about the wedding.'

There was a pause, and when Tara spoke it was in a voice Erin didn't recognise.

'I told him.'

For the second time that day Erin's heart felt as if it had been crushed by an iron fist. For a moment she just sat there frozen with shock, before her breath exploded from her mouth. 'You told him?' she echoed. 'You told Dimitri about the wedding? *You?*'

'Yes,' said Tara.

'What, you just tracked him down and phoned him up and announced that he had a son?'

'He was easy enough to find—he owns half of London, for heaven's sake! Getting through to him was the tricky part but once I mentioned your name, he took the call straight away. But I didn't say anything about Leo, I promise you that, Erin. I just told him you were getting married. I didn't breathe a word about his son.'

'Then how come he knew he had one?'

'*I don't know!*' snapped Tara. 'And before you say anything else—I'm glad I did it. Yes—glad!'

Erin felt sick. Her sister was the closest person she had, next to Leo—the person she would have trusted most in the world—and she had betrayed her to the man she feared most. She had unleashed a powerful secret without knowing where it would take them.

'Why would you be glad about something like that?' she questioned dully.

'You know why,' said Tara softly. 'Because you were breaking the law by marrying Chico so that he could get a work permit and I was worried about the fallout if that ever got out. Because Dimitri might have changed—and shouldn't you at least give him the chance to show you whether he has? But mainly because Leo...'

Her words tailed off and Erin's head jerked back, anger and hurt blending together to form a potent cocktail of emotion as she stared at her sister.

'Because Leo what?' she questioned coldly.

Tara swallowed. 'Leo deserves to know who his father is. He *does*, Erin. Don't you ever feel guilty that he doesn't even *know*?'

'*Of course I do!*' Erin's hissed words were so fervent that they startled her as much as they evidently startled Tara. 'But life isn't black and white. You know exactly why I did it. I didn't want my son to be brought up in the kind of world which Dimitri inhabits.'

'I didn't hear you objecting when you worked for him.'

Erin didn't answer. No, that much was true. Because she'd loved her job and had been dazzled by the trust he'd placed in her. So she'd turned a blind eye to all the whispers and rumours about the Russian oligarch. Even when her eyes had been opened to the kind of man he really was, even when the scales had fallen away and she'd seen the dark soul at his core, it hadn't made any difference. And wasn't that the worst part of all—that she had wanted to reach out to help clear that darkness away instead of running as fast as she could in the opposite direction? What a fool she'd been. Because all that had happened was that her altruism had been misinterpreted by a man who didn't seem to know what kindness was—and had ended up with them having sex. Sex which had meant nothing to him.

'And he's been getting some very good press lately,' continued Tara. 'I'm sure I read that he's built a laboratory to investigate childhood diseases, somewhere in Russia. In fact, I think he's set up some sort of charitable foundation in his name. Maybe he's a reformed character.'

Erin kicked the tip of her white wedding shoe against the counter and for once Tara didn't object. 'Leopards don't change their spots,' she said flatly. 'Everyone knows that.'

'Maybe they don't,' said Tara quietly. 'But even leopards can adapt—otherwise you wouldn't find them living in zoos.'

'I hate zoos,' said Erin, sliding down from the stool and staring at her sister. 'And I still can't believe you told him.'

'I did it because I love you,' said Tara simply. 'And one day you might even thank me for it.'

With an angry shake of her head, Erin went upstairs to the room she shared with Leo. She'd done her best to smarten it up, with pale walls and rows of books which she encouraged her clever son to read—but the cramped dimensions reminded her that this way of living couldn't continue indefinitely. Her gaze lingered on the framed photos of Leo at various milestones in his life—from chubby and very demanding infant right up to his first day of school, last year. She studied that one the hardest, her eyes scanning his innocent little face—so full of hope and happiness—and her heart clenched with a sense of having completely messed things up.

Kicking off her shoes, she changed into her own clothes, wondering how she must have appeared to Dimitri after all these years. Had she changed much? She stared into the mirror. Of course she had. Even the most liberal of observers would have described her appearance as bizarre, and nobody had ever accused Dimitri of being liberal.

Her green eyes were fringed with more makeup than usual and her hair was still woven into a complex updo, studded with the fake-pearl pins which she'd bought from the cash-and-carry to try to emphasise her bridal status. All that time spent angsting over her decision and all the trouble she'd gone to, trying to look like a pukka bride—and it had all been over before it had even begun. Viciously, she tugged the pins out, one by one, until her long brown hair floated free and her thoughts were spinning as she began to brush it.

She had to get a grip. She had agreed on a course of action and she was going to stick to it, with as little fuss and emotion as possible. She would accompany the Russian to Jazratan and pretend to be his secretary. The two of them would talk candidly about Leo and maybe Dimitri would realise that having a child just wouldn't fit into his lifestyle. That there was a good reason why he'd never wanted any children of his own.

And was it a terrible thing to admit that a part of her hoped that would be the case? Because wouldn't that be easier all round? No uneasy meetings. No thoughts about the future. No sizzling sexual chemistry. She put the hairbrush down and gave her reflection a defiant stare.

She would handle it.

She had to.

CHAPTER FOUR

FROM WITHIN THE shadowed interior of the car, Dimitri fixed his gaze on the café opposite. He had been tempted to go inside, to discover what his son's world was really like, but had decided against it—despite his uncanny ability to blend into the background when required. His mouth thinned. Russian men were taught from an early age how to lose themselves in the shadows and he had always managed it better than most, despite his distinctively powerful build and the pale blue eyes he had been told were unforgettable.

He could see Tara standing behind the counter, slicing cheese and making sandwiches. He had met Erin's sister only once before, years ago, and she hadn't seemed to approve of him. Maybe that was why he had been so surprised to receive her phone call. She hadn't been particularly friendly as she'd haltingly explained that Erin was getting married the following week. When he'd asked her outright why she was bothering to tell him, she had refused to be drawn further, but her attitude hadn't bothered him. He was used to women disliking him if they felt he'd taken advantage of them, or, in this case, of their beloved sister. But the fact remained that he had done nothing he was ashamed of. He had taken Erin to bed because she had been practically begging him to and because the chemistry between them had been so explosive that night. Who would ever have guessed that his unassuming little secretary would have been so damned *hot*? Or that she had given him the best sex of his life?

But while her allure had surprised him, he had decided against a repeat performance because he remembered the way she'd made him feel when he had opened his eyes to see her lying beside him. He remembered feeling uncomfortable as her shining gaze had met his. Because this was

Erin. Erin who knew him better than any other woman. Not someone he'd picked up in a nightclub or at a party, but the woman he spent most of his waking hours with. He had felt naked in more ways than one as she had smiled at him dreamily and something unfamiliar had stabbed at his heart. For the first and only time in his life he had realised he couldn't get away with his usual smooth and meaningless post-conquest dialogue. He had broken the rule of a lifetime of mixing work with pleasure and he should have known better.

But Tara's news about her sister's impending wedding had been underpinned with a note in her voice which had alerted his interest. He began to wonder why she'd told him something so seemingly innocuous, when, presumably, legions of his ex-lovers were going off and getting married all the time. There had been something dark and secretive in her tone. Something which had made him pick up the phone to speak with the security firm he had little need of these days.

'Just take a quiet look at a woman called Erin Turner and see what she's up to,' Dimitri had suggested to the head of the firm.

He remembered the expressionless look on the man's face when he had walked into his office a few days later with an envelope which contained a clutch of photos. Photos of a child who looked just like him.

Forcing the memory away, he saw Erin standing in the doorway of the café and watched his driver get out of the car to take her suitcase from her. Dimitri watched as she approached and, inexplicably, his heart began to pound.

She had removed most of the heavy eye make-up she'd been wearing for the wedding and, without the elaborate pearl-studded wedding hairstyle, she looked more like the Erin of old. Her faded jeans were unremarkable and so were her beat-up sneakers. She was wearing a forgettable little waterproof jacket, with some ugly fake fur around the collar, and her long brown hair was tied back in a ponytail, which blew wildly in the strong autumn wind.

His groin grew heavy with lust and Dimitri was irritated by his own reaction, because he didn't understand it. She was ordinary. Some people might have said that she made no effort to attract a man. She didn't dress to impress—clothes had never been high on her list of priorities, even when she'd occupied the prestigious position of being his secretary. So why the sudden urge to crush her lips beneath his and to press himself down on that narrow-hipped body? Was it simply a case of anger being a potent aphrodisiac—or was he remembering that her forgettable looks had been forgotten when she'd come alive in his arms?

The driver opened the door and she got in beside him, a chill breeze accompanying her. He wondered if he was imagining her faint look of disappointment when she saw him sitting in the shadows.

'Hoping I might have changed my mind and left you alone?' he questioned silkily.

Clear green eyes met his. 'Yes,' she said quietly. 'Actually, I was.'

'Sorry to disappoint you, *milaya moya*,' he said sarcastically, and his jaw tightened. 'What time does he get home?'

A look of anxiety crossed her face as she glanced down at her watch. 'Soon. In fact, very soon. We ought to get going.'

Dimitri hesitated as a wave of something he didn't recognise washed over him with a fierce kind of power.

'No,' he said. 'Not yet.'

'He mustn't see me,' she said and suddenly her voice sounded urgent. 'He mustn't.'

'He won't,' he clipped back, impatient now. 'If he looks at anything, it will be at the car, not the passengers. If you're that worried, you can slide down the seat so that you're completely out of view.'

'But why?' she questioned. 'Why risk it?'

Why indeed? Even Dimitri was perplexed by his own reaction. Was it just to convince himself it was true—because he was the kind of man who liked to see the evidence with his own eyes? Or because his love of risk wasn't as deeply buried as he'd thought?

He stretched his fingers out and then bent them so that the knuckles cracked and it sounded almost deafening in the close confines of the car. 'We'll wait five minutes,' he said. 'And if he hasn't appeared by then, we'll go.'

He could feel her tension rising as the minutes ticked by. He could see it in the stiff set of her shoulders and he felt a grim kind of pleasure as she began to shift nervously in her seat. Now might she understand how it felt to be powerless?

'Please, Dimitri,' she said.

But then something in her posture changed—softened—it was like a flower opening to the sun. Following the direction of her gaze, he looked out of the window as a little boy ran along the road with an unknown woman trying to keep up behind him, carrying a plastic lunch box in one hand and a flapping piece of paper in the other.

Dimitri froze as he caught a glimpse of the boy's pale eyes and dark golden hair and bizarrely found his mind flashing back to his own childhood. He remembered the professional photo his parents used to insist on being taken every year on his birthday—stiff-looking portraits where nobody was smiling. There hadn't been a lot to smile about, despite the wealth and the lavish home and the servants.

But this little boy…

His heart clenched.

This little boy was *laughing* as he pushed open the door and disappeared inside the café. His features looked so like Dimitri's own and yet they were completely different—transformed by a wave of sheer happiness.

Dimitri swallowed, but that did nothing to shift the dryness in his throat. He had expected to feel nothing but distance when he first saw the child—and hadn't part of him *wanted* that? He knew how much easier it would be if he could just turn his back and walk away from them both. Erin would doubtless be delighted to see the back of him. And even more delighted not to have to endure two days in a strange country with a man who was still so angry with her. He could speak to his bank and arrange to have the child funded until he was eighteen. If he performed well at school or showed some of his father's natural acumen, there was no reason why he shouldn't be given a role within Dimitri's organisation. And if he proved himself worthy, there was no reason why one day he shouldn't inherit some—maybe all—of Dimitri's vast fortune, for he had never planned for himself the traditional route of marriage and fatherhood.

So why was that impartial assessment not happening? Why was there a stab of something deep in his heart which he couldn't quite define? A feeling of pride and possessiveness, like the day when he'd picked up his first super-yacht—only this was stronger. Much, much stronger.

His breathing wasn't quite steady as he pressed a button recessed in the armrest and the car pulled away.

Erin breathed out a sigh of relief as the café began to retreat into the distance. For one awful moment she'd thought that Leo might see her. Come running over and ask why Mummy was back so early and what was she doing in the big, shiny car with that strange man.

She snatched a glance at Dimitri's profile.

'Thank you,' she said quietly.

'For what?' he demanded.

'For not speaking to him.'

He gave a short and bitter laugh. 'What did you expect me to do—rush up and introduce myself? Hi, Leo, I'm your long-lost daddy!'

'Is that what you wanted to do?'

Dimitri didn't answer. His instinct was to tell her that it was none of her damned business what he wanted to do. But even he could see that it was.

He studied the pale oval of her face and the

green eyes, which were surveying him so steadily. 'No, it's not what I wanted,' he said flatly. 'What I really wanted was to convince myself that it was all some kind of bad dream. That I would look at him and realise there had been some kind of mistake—that you just happen to have a penchant for lovers with hard bodies and high cheekbones and that I was just a number in a possible list of fathers.'

'But now?' she said.

His lips hardened and all the arguments which he might have brought against another woman could not, he realised, be applied to Erin. Because the accusation that she had deliberately fallen pregnant in order to trap him could never be levelled against her. She had not come sniffing around his vast fortune—demanding marriage or regular payments for his son. On the contrary, she had done the exact opposite.

'I don't know,' he said suddenly, in as rare and as honest an admission of confusion as he had ever made—something he could only attribute to the shock of being confronted by his own flesh and blood. 'For while the logical part of my brain continues to tell me I have no desire for a child of my own—there is another part…a part which is more powerful. The part programmed by nature to perpetuate the species. To carry my own, unique genes forward into the future.'

Her face contorted, as if she'd just bitten into something very sour.

'Is that all he is to you, Dimitri—a product of your gene pool?'

'How else do you expect me to react?' he demanded. 'You have given me no opportunity to get to know him. You deny me even the knowledge of his existence. What did you imagine I would feel when I found out, Erin? Only, I was never expected to find out, was I, you cold-hearted little bitch? You would have kept it from me until I had drawn the last breath from my body.'

She flinched. 'I don't want this to deteriorate into a slanging match.'

'At this precise moment I don't particularly care what you want, but you *will* hear me out,' he said icily. 'Do you think I approve of the way you've reared my son? To see him making his home in a place like that?'

'Externals aren't everything,' she flared back defensively. 'And at least I managed to bring him up to be happy and healthy.'

'But you could have done much more than *manage*,' he argued. 'You could have come to me for help. A man who was in a position to help you properly—so that you wouldn't have to struggle bringing up my son in an apartment over a *café* and having to make a sham marriage because you needed money.'

His words brought Erin to her senses. What was she *doing*, letting him browbeat her like this? She knew enough of Dimitri to realise that he would take control in any situation if she let him, because that was his default setting. And she couldn't afford to let him. Not over this.

'You know exactly why I didn't come to you,' she said quietly.

'Because I never wanted children?'

'That was one of the reasons. I…' She halted, suddenly at a loss. *What has Tara done?* she thought bitterly. *What serpent has she unleashed here?*

She swallowed as the enormity of her actions came crashing home in a way it had never done before. Or maybe she had just never allowed herself to think about it properly. She tried putting herself in his shoes and imagining how she would feel if the situation were reversed. Like him, she would be spitting mad and hurt and angry. Had her action of not telling him been motivated simply out of protectiveness for Leo, or had she also been protecting her own vulnerable heart?

Yes.

Yes, she had.

His dark world was not one she wanted her son growing up in. She wanted Leo to remain sunny and innocent—not be dark and complicated like his father. Yet as she looked into Dimitri's proud face she thought she saw a flash of something she didn't recognise in the depths of those icy eyes. Something almost…vulnerable. She gave herself a little shake, telling herself that it was a trick of the light. Because that was a mistake she'd made before. The Russian didn't do vulnerable. He did hard and inviolate and proud.

But none of those facts impacted on the way she was currently feeling—an emotion which felt uncomfortably close to guilt.

'I should have told you,' she said slowly.

He gave the ghost of a smile, as if another small battle had been won. 'Why didn't you?'

Erin shook her head. It was difficult to think straight when he was this close. Tara had told her that she'd rung Dimitri because there was the possibility that he might have changed. *But what if he hadn't?* What if his world was as dark and dangerous as before? And suddenly the truth came blurting out—the memory having the power to hurt her, even now.

'But I did try to tell you. Don't you remember?'

His eyes narrowed and he shook his head. 'When?'

'I came round to your home one Saturday morning, because I felt it best to tell you away from the office. It was just over two months since we'd slept together.' She paused to let her words sink in. 'I suppose it was my own fault. If I'd waited until midday, you might have been alone.'

She had been scared, naïve, foolish, hopeful. It had been ten weeks since she'd spent the night with him. Ten weeks since he'd taken her virginity without realising and then acted as if nothing had happened. He had gone away to Russia on business and then on to the United States. She had suspected that he was deliberately putting distance between them. The weeks had drifted by and her contact with him had been limited to the strictly impersonal. To telephone calls and emails. Clearly he regretted that momentary lapse, which had started with an unexpected kiss and had ended with him thrusting into her over his dining-room table.

She thought at first that her period was late because of the stress and the emotion of having broken the professional boundaries by sleeping with her boss. But her aching breasts were not so easy to ignore. And then she'd missed a second period and had done the test—sitting on the floor of her bathroom and staring at it in disbelief. She knew straight away that she had to tell Dimitri, but she had been so confused. And frightened. She'd blocked out thoughts of how he might react, but one thing she had known above all else was that she wanted to keep this baby. And that her feelings for her boss were secondary to that one fundamental truth.

But Dimitri was away travelling and she was aware she couldn't tell him something like that over the phone, or by email. Apart from anything else, she was terrified it might be intercepted or overheard. On escalating tenterhooks, she waited until he flew in and phoned to say he would be back in the office first thing Monday. She tried to blot out the fact that a new distance seemed to have entered his voice, and that he sounded cool when he spoke to her. And that was when she'd known that she couldn't wait a moment longer and she couldn't tell him at work. She would go round to his apartment and tell him face-to-face, because there was never going to be anything like a 'perfect' time to break the news that she was carrying his baby.

She had—foolishly, in retrospect—gone to a lot of trouble with her appearance that morning. She'd washed her hair and applied a little more make-up than usual. She'd put on a dress, because, she remembered, it had been a sunny spring day—but it hadn't been as warm outside as it had looked from the window of her apartment, and she remembered her bare legs being covered in goosebumps. Afterwards she'd wondered whether she had stupidly been hoping for some romantic conclusion to her news. That he would sweep her into his arms and look down at her with shining eyes, and tell her that it was all going to be okay.

Of course she had.

But he had taken ages to answer the door and, when he had, he had been bad-tempered, sleepy and half naked, his icy eyes narrowed and blood-shot, and his hard jaw shadowed with growth.

'What is it, Erin?' he questioned impatiently, zipping up his jeans with a slight wince. 'Can't it wait?'

She had walked into his apartment, noting the general scene of disarray which greeted her. There was an empty champagne bottle lying on the floor and another which was half drunk—standing on the same table where he had taken her virginity. Now was probably not the right moment to tell him that he was going to be a daddy, but what choice did she have? Tell him on Monday—trying desperately to squeeze in the un-welcome news between wall-to-wall meetings?

It took her a moment or two to notice the vari-ous items of female underwear strewn around the room because she was too busy ogling the lurid cover of what looked like a porn film. She remembered colour flooding to her cheeks as she recalled the picture of a woman wearing very little other than a leather thong and wielding some sort of whip, with a scary look in her eyes. Erin had little experience of men and what they got up to in their leisure time, but even she could work out what had been going on.

And it was then that a woman had appeared from the bedroom, making Erin feel like the biggest fool in the world, because the the woman was completely naked. Her long blonde hair was mussed, her eyes all smudged with mascara and her large breasts jiggled provocatively as she walked into the reception room—completely ignoring Erin—and pouted at Dimitri.

'Aren't you coming back to bed, *lyubimiy*?'

The fact that she was obviously Russian had only made it worse—if it was possible for such a situation to get any more dire than it already was. Erin saw the expression on Dimitri's face—

a mixture of irritation at being interrupted and an unmistakable look of lust, which had automatically darkened his eyes.

'Go back to bed and I'll be there in a minute,' he said, before fixing Erin with an enquiring look. 'So what is it, Erin? What do you want?'

'I…' Erin had been at a loss; her words tailing off until the blonde had wiggled her way back towards the bedroom and she had been momentarily transfixed by the retreating sight of her pale, globe-like buttocks.

'Look.' He paused, as if searching for the right words to say, but of course there *were* no right words. 'I think we both know what happened that night was a mistake and if you were hoping for some kind of repeat—'

'No! No, of course I wasn't,' she said, forcing some stupid, meaningless smile onto her lips as she realised there was only one direction she could contemplate taking. 'I came here to hand in my notice.'

Was that *relief* she saw on his face? Was it?

'You're sure about that?'

Erin nodded. And the fact that he didn't try to talk her out of it spoke volumes. She had fooled herself into thinking she was his indispensable ally—the woman he couldn't do without. And yet she was so wrong. She had become an *embarrassment*, she recognised. The frumpy secretary he'd stupidly bedded in a mad moment when he hadn't been thinking straight. Had he been afraid that she was going to start mooning around after him at the office and becoming a sexual nuisance? Was that why he had uncharacteristically absented himself from England for so long?

'I'd like to leave immediately, if that's okay with you,' she said, as briskly as possible. 'I can easily find someone to step in for me.'

His eyebrows had winged upwards. 'You mean you've had a better offer?'

'Much better,' she lied.

He smiled slightly, as if he understood that. But she guessed he did. Dimitri understood ambition and power and climbing the ladder towards the ever-higher pinnacle of success—it was feelings he was bad at.

But he had made a stab at expressing regret—even if he had done it badly.

'I want you to know that I've…' He shrugged his shoulders and smiled. 'Well, I've enjoyed working with you these past years.'

The easiest thing to have done would have been to have withdrawn gracefully before he probed any further and worked out for himself that there was no other job. Murmured something polite before she walked away for good, so that she could leave on amicable terms. But Erin cared about Dimitri, no matter how much she told herself he didn't deserve it. She had looked into his haunted and sleep-deprived eyes and, although she found herself wishing she could take his unknown pain away, deep down she knew she couldn't save him. He was the only person who could do that. *But didn't she owe him her honesty—if not about her future, then surely about his own? To give him a few home truths, in a way which few other people would ever have dared. To tell him that he might not have a future if he didn't start changing.*

'And I've enjoyed working for you, for the most part,' she said quietly. 'Actually, I used to admire and respect you very much.'

His eyes narrowed, as if he had misheard her. He knitted together the dark eyebrows which contrasted so vividly with the deep gold of his hair. '*Used* to?'

'Sorry to use the past tense,' she said, not sounding sorry at all. 'But it's hard to admire someone who is behaving like an idiot.'

'An *idiot*?' he echoed incredulously.

It hadn't been easy to continue, but she had forced herself to finish what she'd started. 'What else would you call someone who lives the way you do?' she demanded. 'Who goes from day to day on a knife edge, taking all kinds of unnecessary risks? How long do you think your body will survive on too much booze and not enough sleep? How long before your lifestyle impacts on your ability to make razor-sharp business decisions? You're not indestructible, Dimitri—even if you think you are.'

She curled her lips in disgust as she shot the messy room one last withering look—though if he'd been a little more perceptive he might have noticed the distress in her eyes, which had made her start sobbing her heart out the moment she got home to her lovely apartment.

She remembered raising her head from one of the tear-soaked cushions and looking around the luxury home which Dimitri's generous salary had enabled her to rent, knowing that this kind of lifestyle would soon be a thing of the past. Because she wasn't rich and she shouldn't pretend otherwise. She had simply worked for a rich man and now she carried his child beneath her heart while he looked at her with impatient eyes—eager to get back to one of the sexiest women she had ever seen.

'You came round to my apartment and gave

me a piece of your mind,' said Dimitri slowly, his voice breaking into her thoughts and bringing Erin right back to the present. To the luxury car heading towards the city and the man whose icy eyes were boring into her. She looked deep into their pale glitter.

'And found you with another woman,' she said.

Dimitri nodded. Yes, she had found him with another woman. Someone whose face he couldn't even remember, let alone her name. There had been a lot of women like that. One beautiful blonde merging into another, like a blurred and naked merry-go-round whirling through his life and his bedroom.

But he did remember the look of disgust on Erin's face and his instinctive fury that she should dare to judge him. What right did *she* have to judge him? She had made out that she was some paragon of virtue—but she hadn't been so damned virtuous when her nails had been raking his naked back and urging him into her sticky warmth, had she? She had certainly blown her goody-two-shoes image right out of the sky *that* night.

But even though he'd told himself he didn't care what Erin Turner thought about him—he'd found himself thinking about the things she'd said. And there had been a lot of time to consider them during those fruitless months spent seeking a replacement secretary who came even close to her abilities.

His mind cleared as he stared into the clear green light of her eyes.

'And that was enough to prevent you from telling me you were pregnant, was it?' he demanded. 'A simple case of sexual jealousy—because you found me with another woman?'

Erin didn't say anything. Not at first. He made her sound unreasonable—as if she'd simply acted out of pique because her pride had been hurt. But it hadn't just been about the naked blonde. Of much greater concern had been his chaotic lifestyle *which might not have changed*. And if that was the case, she would protect Leo from him with every last breath in her body. She had agreed to spend a weekend with him because she'd been in a position of weakness, but she was not going to be cowed into behaving like a victim. So why not tell him the truth? She had nothing left to lose…

'There was nothing *simple* about it,' she said. 'I didn't want my child to be part of your world.'

His blue eyes were like ice. 'And you were to be the judge and the jury?'

She shrugged. 'Why not? Nobody else ever dared tell you the truth—or if they did, you didn't bother listening to them. Loukas Sarantos told you often enough, before he left your employment.' And suddenly she realised that something else about him was different, and she screwed up her face in confusion as she remembered the eternal shadowy presence which had never been far from his side. 'Where's your bodyguard?' she asked. 'You never go anywhere without a bodyguard.'

'Not any more.' A faint smile lifted the edges of his lips. 'Surprised, Erin?'

'A little.' She nodded. 'Actually, more than a little. What happened?'

He shrugged. 'After Loukas left I could never find anyone else I could bear to have around me 24/7—you know that. And then you left, too.'

Her word fell like a stone into the silence which followed. 'And?'

He glanced out of the window at the stop-start traffic. 'And I realised I was sick of the press dogging my every move and everyone standing on the sidelines waiting for me to tip over the edge.' He turned back to her again. 'So I decided to tie up a few loose ends—actually, more than a few. I cleaned up my act and became Mr Respectable.'

'You?' she echoed. 'Respectable?'

He gave another mirthless smile. 'An image you probably find as difficult to process as much as I do the thought of you as a mother.'

'Touché.' She sighed, wishing she had some kind of magic wand to wave. But if she did, what would she wish for? That she'd never met him? If she wished for that, then she wouldn't have Leo—and she couldn't bear that. 'So what now?' she questioned.

There was a pause as his gaze flicked over her.

'My car is going to drop me off at my office and then it will take you out to the airport, to one of the hotels there. I've had Sofia book you into a suite.'

She looked at him blankly. 'A hotel?'

'Of course. We're flying out first thing and it makes sense for you to be close to the airport. You're masquerading as my secretary, Erin— where else would you go? You can't stay home— and you surely weren't expecting to spend the night with *me*?'

His sarcastic words stung her and made a dull rush of colour stab at her cheeks, but the worst thing of all was that they touched on the truth. *Had* she thought he would be taking her back to that elegant, bonsai-filled apartment of his where there were more than enough spare bedrooms?

Maybe she had—when the truth of it was that since he'd kissed her so coldly yet so passionately in the register office, he hadn't come near her.

She tried to mirror the faint cruelty of his smile. 'Don't be ridiculous, Dimitri,' she said. 'I'm not a complete sucker for punishment.'

CHAPTER FIVE

IT WAS A long time since Erin had stayed in a five-star hotel. Not since she'd worked for Dimitri, when luxury had been the norm. When she'd taken for granted the valets and bellboys and meals which arrived on silent trolleys concealed by heavy silver domes.

Dimitri's car had dropped her off at the Heathrow branch of the Granchester hotel chain, which was tucked away only ten minutes' drive from Heathrow. True, her suite didn't have the greatest view in the world but the bathroom was every woman's fantasy. After stripping off all her clothes, she lost herself in a world of scented bubbles and dried her hair and was just padding around in the oversized towelling robe, when the doorbell rang.

At first she thought it might be the soup and salad she'd ordered from room service, but instead she found Dimitri's assistant, Sofia, standing there, her arms laden down with glossy bags and shoe boxes.

'Dimitri said you'd need these,' she said as Erin invited her in.

Erin stared at the bags in confusion. 'What are they?'

'Clothes suitable for staying in a country with clothing restrictions a little more rigid than our own.'

Erin nodded. She guessed what Sofia meant was that her own everyday clothes would be completely unsuitable for a stay in a royal palace. Her ordinary jeans and sweaters and dresses—bought in chain stores or online—would highlight a relative poverty which might reflect badly on Dimitri. If she was supposed to be the secretary to one of the world's richest men, it followed she would need to look the part. Erin watched as Sofia pulled a full-length fitted gown from one of the bags and gave an instinctive little murmur of pleasure.

'How did you know my size?' she questioned as she leaned forward to touch it, her fingertips skating over the exquisitely embroidered silk dress.

'I had a rough idea from the way my jeans fitted you—or didn't fit you!—but it was Dimitri who guessed,' answered Sofia, with a slightly embarrassed shrug.

Erin gave a wry smile. Of course he had guessed. With the amount of women Dimitri had bedded, he could probably work out a woman's measurements to within the nearest centimetre.

Sofia left soon after and Erin picked at a supper she didn't really want, before getting into the largest and softest bed she'd ever seen. Except that she couldn't sleep. She kept thinking back over the things Dimitri had said. The way he'd described himself as Mr Respectable and her natural reluctance to believe him. Or maybe she didn't *dare* believe him. Because how could a red-blooded sinner like him suddenly become a bona fide saint?

The hotel was deathly quiet and she glanced at her watch and grimaced. Three-fifteen in the morning. Picking up the TV's remote control, she put on the rolling news summary. Bright pictures appeared on the giant screen and she lay there listening to the drone of the announcer until she must have dropped off, because she awoke to the sound of her phone ringing.

It was Sofia, telling her that the car was waiting outside to take her to the airport and that Dimitri would meet her there.

'And I hope...' Sofia hesitated. 'I hope you have a lovely vacation in Jazratan.'

'Vacation' wouldn't have been Erin's word of choice as one of Dimitri's powerful jets thundered down the runway and soared up into the cloudless autumn sky. And she didn't feel remotely vacation-like when the plane touched down on Jazratan soil eight hours later. They had exchanged few words during the long flight, but that hadn't stopped her from being uncomfortably aware of his presence. Especially when he'd first seen her in the full-length embroidered dress, which made walking more difficult than usual. The soft silk revealed no flesh whatsoever, but Erin had felt almost naked as those blue eyes burned into her.

She hated the way her body tingled in response, as if it were written into her DNA that she should desire him every time he looked at her with hunger in his eyes…

She'd tried to read a magazine, wondering if he was aware that she wasn't taking in a single word. She found herself ridiculously grateful when he fell asleep and for once his hard face softened. And even though she'd tried not to, it had been impossible not to drink in the carved beauty of his proud features—until one of the stewards had appeared and she'd been forced to hastily avert her gaze.

Her body felt stiff as the aircraft doors were pushed open and her sense of detachment only increased when she saw the deputation of robed figures waiting to greet them. Nervously, she smoothed down her hair, which had already begun to react to the dense blanket of heat which hit them the moment they stepped outside. The burning heat and the vivid blue sky were so different from the drizzle she'd left back at home in England, and she'd never gone away without Leo before. She thought about her son back in London and felt a sudden pang as she turned to Dimitri. The desert sun was gilding his hair into an abundance of deepest gold and she thought his eyes had never looked quite so blue. 'I must ring Leo.'

'I think it had better wait until we have reached the royal palace,' he said. 'There's a certain amount of protocol we need to get through before you start pulling out your cell phone.'

This can't be happening, Erin thought as she was ushered into the first of a convoy of vehicles by the light press of Dimitri's hand at her spine. *I can't be in an air-conditioned car so cold that it feels like travelling in an icebox, while outside there are palm trees and camels carrying men with headdresses billowing behind them as they move across the dusty sands.*

But it *was* happening. Every surreal second of it. People were bowing as the convoy went past—as if they suspected that their royal king might be enclosed in one of the long line of dark vehicles. The car was approaching an enormous domed palace whose golden gates were opening before them. Past stern-faced guards they drove, into vast and formal grounds, studded with marble statues and exotic blooms she'd never seen before. She found herself wondering how on earth the grass could be so green when nothing but dust and desert surrounded them. She wondered what kind of birds she could hear singing in those strange and beautiful trees.

'Excited?' came the accented caress of Dimitri's voice from beside her as they came to a halt.

She turned to look at him, hating the instant thudding of her heart. Why did it have to be *him* who made her body react like this? Why couldn't she have desired some other man to tease her bare breasts with his teeth, as Dimitri had done on that long-ago night she'd never forgotten.

'I don't know if "excited" is the word I'd use,' she answered, trying to sound blasé. 'It will be an interesting experience to see a country I would never normally get the chance to visit—but the thought of being cooped up with you for two days isn't exactly filling me with joy.'

'Oh, really?' he drawled, knotting his silk tie as he glanced towards the palace doors. 'And fascinating as this discussion is, I think we're going to have to take a rain check. Because if you look over there you'll see a man in golden robes heading this way. It seems that the Sheikh of Jazratan has come out in person to greet us.'

'I notice that you have been very preoccupied tonight, my friend.'

Dimitri smiled as he listened to the Sheikh's silken words, for they both knew that the title of 'friend' was completely spurious. The man who said it was too remote and too powerful to have true friends—indeed, Saladin was as friendless as he, for men like them always stood alone.

But that was the way he liked it.

Dimitri watched as yet another fragrant platter of food was placed before him, waiting until the robed male servant had withdrawn, before turning to the hawk-faced king beside him.

'Have I?'

'Mmm.' The Sheikh waved away another servant who was hovering with a water jug. 'I note that you have barely been able to tear your gaze away from your *secretary* all evening.'

Dimitri picked up a jewel-inlaid goblet and sipped from it. 'Is it not always the instinct of a man to look at a woman, particularly when she is the only one present?'

'Indeed it is,' commented Saladin thoughtfully, his eyebrows rising to just below the edge of his white headdress. 'But she does not fall into the category of your preferred blondes, one of whom

I saw pictured with you in the newspapers not a fortnight ago.'

Dimitri gave a thin smile. 'You surprise me, Saladin. I did not have you down as a reader of tabloid newspapers.'

The Sheikh's eyes hardened. 'Ah, but I always do my research. I like to know about the lifestyle of my prospective business partners.'

Dimitri put his goblet down, his heart giving a quick beat—as if sensing that, after so many years of delicate negotiation, the prize was at last within his grasp. But he kept all emotion from his voice. 'Do I take it this means you have agreed to sell me the oil fields?'

A shadow of something imperceptible moved across Saladin's hawklike features.

'I try never to conduct business at mealtimes,' he said smoothly. 'It has been a long day and your secretary is looking somewhat *weary*. I trust that your sleeping arrangements meet with your satisfaction?'

Dimitri stiffened, wondering what Saladin was

hinting at. Had he suspected that he and Erin had once been lovers and might have preferred a shared suite rather than the two adjoining ones they'd been allocated? No. He felt the flicker of a pulse at his temple. One unplanned night all those years ago did not put them in the category of *lovers*. It had been nothing. Nothing but a blip. He drank some more pomegranate juice. And yet he had never been able to completely forget that night, had he? It had been too easy to recall the way he'd felt as he had thrust deep inside her. The memory of her slim-hipped body and tiny breasts was curiously persistent. It was forbidden fruit at its sweetest.

He saw Saladin watching her and felt a responding shimmer of something which felt decidedly *territorial*. The mother of his child was sitting between Prince Khalim of Maraban and the ambassador of nearby Qurhah, looking almost as if she had been born to eat from jewelled platters, in the sumptuous opulence of a state banqueting room.

It was an image he found difficult to reconcile, because this was not the Erin he knew. She had always been such a *back room* type of person, content to apply herself industriously at the office and fade into the fixtures and fittings. Unlike other members of his staff, she had never hankered after the glamour of the high-profile parties and events he was regularly invited to.

Had he thought she might seem out of her depth here, in such imposing and opulent surroundings—where chandeliers like cascades of diamonds dangled from the ceilings, and intricate mosaic work made the walls look as if they were fashioned from pure gold? Because if that was the case, then he had been wrong.

Tonight she seemed to have an innate grace about her which he'd never really noticed when she'd been sitting behind a desk, fielding his phone calls. Her wrists were so damned *delicate*, he thought, watching as she lifted a jewel-studded goblet to her lips and sipped from it. The residue of the drink left a faint gleam on her lips and he found himself noticing how perfect they looked.

He narrowed his eyes. What was the matter with him tonight? What was it about her which made her seem so…*bewitching*? Surely it couldn't just be that silvery-green gown, which made her body gleam like a mermaid and brought out the colour of her eyes. He wondered what she was saying to that Qurhahian which had made him throw back his dark head and laugh so much.

At that moment she seemed to sense his eyes on her, because slowly she turned her head and met his steady gaze. And something about the stillness which settled over her made the rest of the room suddenly retreat. The sounds of chatter became muffled and all Dimitri could hear was the sound of his own heartbeat. With a start, he realised that she looked almost *beautiful*.

His fingers tightened around his goblet. Whoever would have guessed that Erin Turner could look so at home in this regal setting? That in spite of the maelstrom of events which had led to her being here, she had somehow maintained an air of calm and dignity, which she was carrying off with aplomb?

He could feel the urgent jerk of his erection and wondered if he was imagining the tightening of her nipples in response to his scrutiny, or whether that was simply his own fantasy running wild. He felt a momentary pang of regret as he realised that he hadn't enjoyed Erin Turner as a woman should be enjoyed. His desire for her had been raw and unfamiliar. A one-off he'd found difficult to understand—both at the time and afterwards. But it had been at a dark time in his life, hadn't it? Just about the time when he'd reached his rock-bottom, and Erin had witnessed every second of it.

He had seen the look of alarm in her eyes when she'd arrived at his apartment that night. A look which had given away to relief when he'd eventually answered the door and she realised that he'd been delayed by nothing more onerous than a shower. He remembered feeling weary—and jaded. He'd spent the previous night in a casino, being fawned over by women wearing nothing but a smattering of sequins, but Erin had looked so young and so *fresh* in that boxy navy work suit that desire had suddenly taken root inside him. And once it had been planted, it had grown like something rampant and uncontrollable.

He had kissed her more as an experiment than anything else—expecting a prim response or even a slap round the face for daring to make a pass at her. But it hadn't turned out that way. She had kissed him back—with a passion which had more to do with enthusiasm than experience, and it had blown him away. He hadn't planned to pull her into his arms and God only knew how they had ended up on his dining-room table, with him ripping off her panties and her urging him on with a gurgle of delighted laughter. He remembered his shuddered shout of pleasure as he had cased himself into her tight and sticky warmth.

But the sex had only been the beginning and he

hadn't liked what had come afterwards. Daylight had brought with it disbelief. It had felt *claustrophobic* to wake up in Erin's arms. He had felt uncomfortable beneath that sweet, uncomplicated gaze of hers. His decision to fly unexpectedly to Russia had been dramatic but necessary, because she'd made him feel stuff. Stuff he hadn't wanted to feel—and it was easier to escape from it than to confront it.

A robed servant removed his untouched dessert and replaced it with a cup of mint tea and suddenly Dimitri couldn't wait for dinner to end as he realised he wanted sex with Erin Turner again. His mouth dried. He wanted a replay of what had happened all those years ago, only this time he wanted to do it long and slow.

He shook his head as he tried to fight the hungry demands of his body. Because this was the woman who deceived him. The woman who had decided to play judge and jury and to hide his child from him, without ever giving him the opportunity to show her he'd changed. He thought of another woman who had done something similar and he felt his heart twist with a cold anger.

He realised that the Sheikh was speaking to him and forced himself to listen.

'You must be weary after your travels, Makarov?'

'A little,' Dimitri agreed.

'Then we will retire for the night, since negotiations are better conducted by the light of day, following a good night's sleep and a little exercise.' The Sheikh smiled. 'I believe you ride?'

'Of course,' said Dimitri.

'Then perhaps you would care to join me in the morning?' The Sheikh's eyes gleamed. 'I have two fine new stallions I am keen to show you and to put through their paces.'

Dimitri gave a little click of irritation. 'I would like nothing better but have brought no riding clothes with me.'

'This is of no matter.' The Sheikh gave an impatient wave of his hand. 'I can provide you with something. We are men of similar size, I think.

Meet me at eight—before the sun is too high and the desert heat becomes merciless. And in the meantime I shall bid you and your secretary a good night.' The Sheikh rose to his feet and everyone fell silent as he swept from the room, followed by a retinue of servants.

As the chatter recommenced Dimitri stood up and walked round the other side of the table, where Erin was giggling at something the Qurhahian official was saying. Was that what made Dimitri clamp a possessive hand over her arm, or simply that the desire to touch her had become too strong to resist?

'*Zvezda moya*, you have spent many hours travelling today,' he said, seeing the faint clouding of her eyes which she couldn't quite disguise. As if it was hypocritical of him to use the Russian term of endearment, or to whisper his fingertips over her slamming pulse like that. Unseen, he circled his thumb over the delicate skin and he felt her heart pick up even more speed. 'Let us follow the Sheikh's good example and retire for the night.'

Erin nodded as she stood up and said goodnight to the interesting ambassador from Qurhah, who had told her so many interesting things about living in the desert. She would never have guessed in a million years that the way to stop yourself feeling thirsty was to suck on a pebble, or that cacti had so many medicinal uses. In a way she was reluctant to leave the table, but she could hardly sit there all night just because she was terrified about the thought of being alone with Dimitri. Especially after the way he had been ogling her during dinner.

And the way her body had instinctively responded to him. That was what was worrying her more than anything. She'd tried to rationalise it as best she could, but in the end she'd been forced to face the truth. That she still wanted him. She swallowed. But that didn't mean she was going to follow through. Because even though she'd ring-fenced her heart, Dimitri could still mess

with her head. He could make her want things
she knew were bad for her.

Mainly him.

Walking rigidly alongside him, she attempted
to concentrate on her surroundings as they left
the banqueting hall, trying to steer her thoughts
away from his power and strength. But it wasn't
easy. There was a definite *edge* to him tonight.
An edge which was all about sex—she guessed
that, despite her relative innocence. The hunger
in his eyes had been unmistakable as he'd stared
at her across the dinner table—and she couldn't
deny that the feeling had been mutual. She had
been overcome with a breathless need to feel him
close to her again. To have him crush his lips
down on hers. To let him pin her down onto the
mattress and…and…

Erin swallowed.

And it wasn't going to happen.

It *couldn't* happen.

Because sex with Dimitri would weaken her.
It would tear down her defences and make her

helpless. And she couldn't afford to be helpless. For Leo's sake, she had to stay strong.

He might have changed in many ways. He might no longer be gambling, or drinking or embracing danger with a reckless hunger—but there was no guarantee that his attitude towards women was any different. *Remember the way he treated you.* She certainly hadn't been expecting violins and commitment from him, but after that single night of sex he had been barely able to look her in the eyes. He'd acted as if the whole extraordinary night had never happened.

Her sandals made little sound as they made their way along the marbled corridors. But the magnificent architecture and scented courtyards were wasted on her—just like the wrought-iron lamps which flickered delicate patterns onto the walls. Her mind started picturing her little apartment back home, where everything she held dear was centred. She thought about a little boy sitting at a table, crayoning. She thought about his warm milk and bedtime story and those innocent eyes, which were so like those of his manipulative father, and her heart clenched.

They reached her suite first and stopped outside and Erin felt slightly breathless as she pushed open the door. Inside, low divans were scattered with brocade cushions and the powerful scent of roses wafted through the air.

'Goodnight,' she said, thinking how inadequate that word sounded when all she could think about was that he was close enough to touch. Close enough to kiss. *So go. Go now—before the cool gleam of his eyes entices you any more and the sensual lines of his lips tempt you into doing something you shouldn't.* But her sandaled feet didn't move from the spot.

Dimitri stared at the woman in front of him, conscious of the mixed messages she was sending out, and conscious of his own feelings of confusion. He wanted to remember the web of deceit she had woven and to remind himself that she'd told the same lies as his own, dear mother. But the hungry throb of desire which pulsed through his body was far stronger than his reservations. Part of him hated what he was about to do, but he seemed unable to stop himself from stepping onto the inevitable path of seduction. 'You look beautiful tonight, Erin.'

She looked momentarily nonplussed, as if she wasn't used to receiving compliments about her looks. 'Thank you,' she said, her voice betraying a hint of nerves. 'I have Sofia to thank for the dress. She has excellent taste.'

'I don't want to talk about Sofia's taste.'

'No,' she said, looking as if she was trying to make herself yawn. 'Actually, it's very late and I want to go to sleep—'

'Are you quite sure about that?' he questioned.

'About…what? About whether I want to go to sleep?'

'About what you really want.' He reached out to touch her cheek. 'See how you shiver when I touch you?'

'Maybe I'm cold.'

'In the desert?'

She licked her lips. 'Dimitri,' she whispered. 'Don't.'

'Don't what? Don't tell it how it is, when I get the distinct feeling that you want me as much as I want you. Don't you? I think you want me to kiss you—and God knows I want that, too. You've driven me crazy all through dinner. I could barely concentrate on a word the Sheikh was saying because I kept looking at you and thinking how much I longed to touch you.'

His words disarmed her and so did the molten look of desire in his eyes—and Erin was already weakened by her own desire and the stupid vulnerability which his passionate words had stirred up. Was that to blame for what happened next—so quickly and so completely that any other action seemed unthinkable? One minute she was staring at him and trying to summon up the strength to walk away and the next she was in his arms and he was kissing her so hungrily that she thought she gasped, or squealed or *something*.

Perhaps the sound reminded him that they were on the Sheikh's territory and the rules governing Jazratan were far stricter than their own, because suddenly Dimitri was levering her into her suite and shutting the door behind them. For a moment she just stared at him with her heart beating wildly beneath the beautiful dress and then he was pushing her up against the wall and kissing her.

One last stab at reason told her to stop him before it was too late, but she simply ignored it, coiling her arms greedily around his neck as he deepened the kiss. Because he was right. Her eyelids flickered to a close as his tongue began to explore her mouth. She *did* still want him.

For years she'd been yearning for his kiss—not the arrogant mark of possession which had taken place in the register office, but this. A *real* kiss.

When she'd lain sleepless, with his baby kicking beneath her heart, she had wanted him to hold her tight like this. In those early years of struggle, when she'd discovered that Leo was allergic to peanuts and she'd felt as if she'd been running round chasing her tail, existing on hardly any sleep and far too much black coffee, she had longed for the comfort of a man's touch.

Dimitri's touch.

And now she had it—and it was all-consuming. He was driving his lips down hard on hers and she was responding in kind, not just because she felt frustrated and empty or because he was irresistible—it went much deeper than that. Because their cells had mingled when their child had formed inside her and Dimitri had awoken her in so many ways. He had taken her virginity and given her an orgasm and made her pregnant, all during one long night of bliss.

His hands were moving over her body, palms undulating over the narrow curves of waist and hips, as if he were discovering them for the first time. She heard his low growl of pleasure as he brought her up against the growing hardness at his groin, mirrored by the molten rush of heat to her sex. He cupped one of her breasts, curling his fingers over the shiny green material, and her nipple pushed insistently against his palm as she teetered on the brink of giving in to the urgent demands of her body. A couple of minutes more and he would be undressing her. He would be kissing his way over her naked body and she would be urging him on, just like last time.

Until the truth hit her like a bucket of ice water as she realised what he was doing. Once again, she was letting him *use* her. She had dressed up for dinner and behaved as impeccably as she knew how and he was responding by behaving as if she were nothing more than a decorative object he could take to bed without conscience. As if she were a piece of clay he could mould to his own desires, never stopping to think that she might have *feelings*—and that he might be trampling all over them.

Tearing her lips away from his, she used all her strength to plant her hands on his shoulders to push him away and he jerked his head back in surprise.

His eyes darkened. 'What's wrong?'

She stepped away from him and the temptation he presented. She could feel the heat of her face and the thunder of her pulse as she glared at him. 'What's wrong? Are you…serious?' she demanded breathlessly. 'Do you really think you can walk back into my life and completely disrupt it—and then expect me to have sex with you, just because you've snapped your fingers?'

'But you want me.'

He said it unequivocally—like someone stating calmly that the sky was blue—and all the anger which had been simmering away inside Erin now came to the boil.

'Oh, I might *want* you,' she agreed. 'My body may have been programmed to react to yours in a way I don't particularly like, but that doesn't mean I'm going to follow through. Because you don't have any respect for women, do you, Dimitri? Not just me, but any woman. You use your undoubted charisma to get them into your bed, but you blaze through their lives without thinking about the consequences. You used me that night because you were in a dark place—and afterwards you just cast me aside, as if I was someone of no consequence. Like I was a *thing*—not a person.'

She shook her head as she struggled to get more breath in her lungs. 'I thought my sister was wrong to tell you about my wedding—but now I can see it was probably the right thing to do. Leo does have the right to know about his father. But that doesn't mean I'm going to act like…like some sort of *convenience* by getting intimate with you. Because that night was a one-off and it was a mistake.'

'Erin—'

'No! You aren't going to change my mind—no matter how hard you try.' Frustratedly she pushed a handful of hair away from her hot face. 'While we're here we can accomplish what we initially set out to do. I will pretend to be your secretary if that's what you want and we can use the time to decide on a way forward best suited to our son. But I don't plan on having sex with you, Dimitri—not now and not ever—so you'd better get that into your stubborn head.'

CHAPTER SIX

DIMITRI'S BODY ACHED and his blood sang with the most unbearable frustration he'd ever experienced. He still couldn't quite believe the way the evening had ended—with Erin refusing to have sex with him, even though her body had been screaming out its objections as she'd pushed him away.

When had a woman ever done that?

Walking over to the unshuttered windows, he stared out at the clear night sky of Jazratan. With no light pollution, the stars were impossibly bright and they shone down over the desert plains like blazing beacons. He had left the bedroom windows open and the scent of the exotic blooms in the palace gardens drifted in to mingle with the heavy fragrance of the roses which perfumed the room. It was over two hours since she'd kicked him out of her suite and yet still he couldn't sleep.

In the old days he might have seen off a shot or three of vodka to chase away the uncomfortable feelings which now gnawed away at the pit of his stomach. If he'd been in a city, he might have ordered a car to drive him to a casino, where he would play cards until daybreak. But it was nearly seven years since he'd drunk vodka or gambled away his money, and so far he hadn't missed either.

Until tonight.

Tonight he would have welcomed the oblivion of something—anything—to blot out these dark thoughts. What he wouldn't give to forget the accusations she'd flung at him, or to work out why they had cut so deep.

Because they were true?

He stared into the sky as a shooting star shot through the inky stratosphere, leaving behind a blurred and silvery trail. *Had* he treated her like a commodity by kicking her out of his apartment the morning after he'd bedded her—or had he simply been protecting her from the kind of man he really was? He hadn't wanted to drag someone like Erin into the seedy world he'd inhabited at the time. He had looked into her shining eyes and known that he couldn't take away any more of her innocence. She deserved better than him.

He'd convinced himself that he was doing her a favour by making it clear that if she wanted to hold on to her job, they must resume their roles of boss and employee. That was why he'd left the country—to give her time to get used to the fact that the sex wasn't going to happen again. And when he'd returned she had come round to his apartment with that strange expression on her face and had found him *in flagrante* with some blonde. He'd thought sexual jealousy had been the motivation behind her decision to resign—and in many ways it had been simpler to let her go. He hadn't wanted to be reminded of the night they'd shared. He hadn't wanted to

have to fight off any inconvenient feelings of still
wanting her...

But the truth was that he'd missed her. No secretary he'd employed before or since had been
able to equal her. They'd always worked well
together—even if sometimes she used to regard him sternly with those catlike eyes of hers.
He had allowed Erin Turner a cautious proximity which nobody other than his most favoured
bodyguard had been granted. And the irony of
it was that he'd never even thought about her in
a sexual way before that night. To him she'd just
been part of the background—as reliable as the
cup of strong coffee she placed on his desk each
morning. Sometimes they used to discuss the
morning's headlines. Sometimes he used to ask
her opinion and, occasionally, act on it. Was it
a crazy admission to make that he'd almost *forgotten* she was a woman, until the night when
his spirit had been dark and desperate and she
had been standing in his doorway in her sensible

navy work suit. He had looked at her and suddenly she had been *all* woman.

He thought about her sleeping in the adjoining suite as dawn broke over the Jazratan desert in an explosion of colour—turning the sky an intense shade of rose pink before giving way to gold, then amber. But suddenly his thoughts were far away from the luxurious palace. He thought about the laughing little boy he'd seen running along the London street and his heart clenched with an emotion he didn't recognise.

He showered and shaved, but Erin still hadn't risen when a servant rapped at the door and presented him with a folded pile of riding clothes. Minutes later, he emerged from his dressing room to see that she must have let herself into his suite while he'd been changing. She was staring out at the gardens and she was washed gold with morning sunlight, wearing another of those all-concealing outfits—the ones deemed suitable not to offend the country's notoriously strict dress codes, but which somehow managed to draw attention to the slender curves of her body. She turned round when she heard him enter and, although her face looked bloodless and pale, he couldn't miss the way her eyes darkened when she saw him.

Infuriatingly, he felt his body's own powerful response to her presence but, ruthlessly, he clamped it down. Because it was better this way. In the cold, clear light of morning it was easier to compartmentalise the lust he'd felt for her last night and to squash it. Far better they kept things businesslike and impersonal.

'Ah, awake at last,' he remarked non-committally. 'I trust you slept well?'

Erin met his cool gaze with a feeling of confusion. She had anticipated that this morning's conversation was going to be difficult in view of what had nearly happened last night, and would need careful handling. She had planned to stick to neutrals—to concentrate on the banal and not give in to all the dark thoughts which were jostling for space inside her head. She had intended to forget last night's kiss and all the hungry feelings it had provoked, but the look on Dimitri's face told her she needn't have worried. It seemed that her concerns about having to resist him again were completely unfounded—because he was looking at her as dispassionately as he might look at a speck of dust on his shirt.

Yet the sight of him striding into the room wearing riding gear was doing dangerous things to her heart rate. Why was he dressed in a way which was so unbelievably provocative? The jodhpurs did things to his body which were only just this side of decent, clinging to every sinew of his muscular thighs and hugging his hips like a second skin. A billowing white silk shirt was tucked into the waistband and hinted at the hard torso which lay beneath. Dark leather knee-length boots completed the outfit and Erin could feel her mouth growing dry because suddenly he looked like every woman's fantasy. And she had turned him down...

Was she insane?

She cleared her throat. 'What…what are you doing?'

'Isn't it obvious?' he said, with a touch of impatience in his voice. 'I'm getting ready to go riding with the Sheikh.'

'You didn't mention that last night.'

'Why? Should I have run it past you first?'

'Don't be ridiculous,' she said, unable to quell her natural concerns for him, even though he was stonewalling every remark she made. 'When was the last time you rode?'

'Why?'

She shrugged, but she could feel the familiar flare of fear leaping up inside her.

He seemed so different these days. So cool and in control. A long way from the man who'd never slept—who'd existed on vodka and danger. And now he was putting himself in danger again. He was acting like arrogant, invulnerable Dimitri once more. The man who thought he was charmed—but how long before his charmed life ran out?

She glared at him, resenting the way he was making her feel. *She didn't want to worry about him any more, or fret about him. Those days were over and what he did was none of her business.* But something made her say it anyway. Was it the thought of Leo and something happening to the daddy he would only just be getting to know? Or was the shameful truth that she was getting in much deeper than she'd imagined and the thought of something happening to him more than she could bear?

'It's dangerous.'

'Only if you don't know what you're doing—and I do. I learned to ride in the Russian army on the famous Don horse—the favoured mount of the Cossacks. Remember?' His eyes glinted out a challenge. 'I've been well taught, Erin—you know that—and I respect the might and the power of the horse, ever to be flippant about riding one. I do have *some* redeeming qualities, even if last night you seemed determined to list all my negative ones.'

She bit her lip, wondering if some of the accusations she'd hurled at him had been unduly harsh.

'Last night.' She cleared her throat. 'Those things I said—'

'Were probably things I needed to hear.' His eyes glittered. 'Because most of the things you said were true, and I'm sorry.'

She met his gaze with suspicion and confusion, because contrition was not an emotion she'd ever associated with Dimitri Makarov.

'Oh,' she said, unable to keep the faint note of surprise from her voice. 'Right.'

'I've taken on board that you don't want any intimacy with me, Erin,' he said. 'And with hindsight—I think that may be the best decision.'

Even more confused now, Erin looked at him. 'You do?'

'I do. Last night happened for all kinds of reasons, but I'm grateful to you for stopping it in time. Starting a physical relationship creates its own kind of tension between a couple—particularly when it comes to an end. And I think Leo deserves more than his parents warring.'

Now Erin felt completely wrong-footed. 'You sound...'

Golden-brown eyebrows winged upwards. 'What?'

She shrugged, unsure how much to say and unwilling to threaten this tentative truce. But last night seemed to have opened up a new channel of communication and maybe it was time to start dealing permanently in the currency of truth. She'd seen the trouble subterfuge could cause and if their uneasy partnership of shared parentage was to have any kind of future, then they needed to be honest with each another. And if sex was off the agenda, they could concentrate on the other stuff. The important stuff.

But that didn't stop her from being curious. From wondering what made him tick.

'You make it sound as if you think every physical relationship will end,' she said.

'That's because they do. And if they survive,

they are invariably riddled with infidelity. And there's no need to look at me quite so disapprovingly, Erin. I've never made any secret of my cynicism. You should know that better than anyone.'

'I do.' She hesitated. 'It's just I've never known *why*.'

'It wouldn't take a genius to work it out.' His voice roughened. 'Don't they say that the first relationship you observe is the blueprint for your own life?'

'You mean your parents weren't happy?'

'No, they weren't,' he said, but he quickly followed up his answer with another question, as if eager to change the subject. 'Though I suppose your childhood was all milk and honey and picnics on the weekend?'

'Well, that's what my parents were aiming for,' she said, watching as he picked up his riding crop to twist it between his fingers. 'Only, my perfect childhood didn't turn out the way it was supposed to. If ever we had picnics, then the sandwiches were jam and the bread was stale, because there was never enough money to go round.'

'Why not?'

She sighed. 'Because my parents were impossible romantics. They've spent their lives following the demands of their hearts, but never bothered listening to their heads. They live in Australia now. They went there after seeing a documentary on ostrich farming and decided to start up a farm of their own. They were seduced by big blue skies and a hot sun and the idea of being close to the earth—without stopping to think that a little bit of farming experience might be a good idea before they actually channelled all their savings into it.'

His eyes narrowed. 'What happened?'

She shrugged. 'What everyone told them would happen, only they were too stubborn to pay any attention. They lost all their money and the farm was repossessed—and now my mother has had the bright idea of making silver jewellery, at a time when mass-market products are in the ascendancy, so nobody is buying hers. They are currently travelling around New South Wales in a camper van, selling her wares in markets and barely making enough money to make ends meet.'

He was silent for a minute. 'And what do these two impossible romantics think of Leo?' he asked suddenly. 'Do they mind you having a child out of wedlock? Are they close to their grandson?'

She shook her head. 'No, they're not close to him—at least, not geographically. We email and talk via the internet once a week, but it's not quite the same thing. They can't afford to come to England and I was only able to afford to fly out there once. That was...' She hesitated.

His eyes narrowed.

'That was another reason why you decided to marry Chico, wasn't it? So that you could afford to visit them more often?'

'That's right.' His perception surprised her. 'I thought they'd be pleased but they...'

'They what?'

His unfamiliar interest in her personal life was beguiling, but it was making her think about stuff it was better to avoid. Her parents had wanted her and Tara to marry for love because they believed in love. She did not. She believed in providing security and protection for yourself because love was flaky and unreliable. It made people make stupid, random decisions like going off to the other end of the world, fuelled by nothing but a pipe dream, just as they had done.

But once she had believed in love, hadn't she? She had been sucked in by that meaningless fairy tale, just like everyone else. She'd misinterpreted her boss's relaxed attitude towards her and thought it might be something else. Her feelings for him had bubbled away, getting hotter and hotter. By the time he'd kissed her that night in his apartment, all her immunity had gone—and she realised too late that she could never get it back again. Before, she had been Erin his trusted aide…and afterwards?

Afterwards, she had been just another woman

he'd bedded. Just another woman he couldn't wait to see the back of, scrabbling around on the floor to locate her scattered underwear. But at least she had one thing to thank Dimitri for. With one stroke he had effectively destroyed the love myth which had been building up inside her. As she'd walked home that morning, wearing last night's clothes, she had vowed she would never be like her parents.

Never.

She shook her head. 'They think that babies should only be the product of love. And even if that patently isn't true—I don't want that kind of love.'

'You don't want love?' he echoed slowly. 'Why not?'

'Because it takes over your life.' She shook her head impatiently. 'I've seen what it does to people—the way my parents allowed it to dominate their lives, so that nothing else really mattered. I've seen it break hearts and cause jealousy. It's nothing but a con. A way of justifying desire, that's all. Now who's the one looking shocked? What's the matter, Dimitri? Do you think all women are programmed to lose their hearts to a man?'

He didn't take the bait. 'Going back to your parents, do they know I'm the father of your child?'

She shook her head. 'No. Nobody does, except Tara.'

'So why not? Why the desire for secrecy? You could have taken the story to the press,' he observed. 'You could have earned yourself a nice little payout without having to resort to a sham marriage.'

'I would never do that,' she said fiercely. 'That kind of cheap publicity is the last thing I would inflict on Leo.'

He regarded her thoughtfully. 'But there was another reason for your discretion, wasn't there, Erin? Because if you'd gone to the press—I would inevitably have found out and that was something you didn't want to risk, did you?'

Erin stared at him as the silence seemed to expand the space between them. She heard the hurt and the anger in his voice, knowing both were justified, and the stab at her conscience was almost more than she could bear. 'You're right,' she said in a low voice. 'I wanted to keep him hidden away from you.'

She hardly dared look at him to see his reaction, but she knew that to avert her gaze would be the act of an emotional coward. She wondered if she had imagined that brief, hard flare of *sadness* in his eyes, when she had been expecting the full force of his anger.

'It's history now,' he said abruptly as he glanced down at his watch. 'It's nearly eight o'clock. Are you coming to watch me ride?'

Erin hesitated. The conversation had left her feeling raw and exposed—but what else was she going to do if he went off to ride with the Sheikh? Sit alone in her suite while crazy thoughts circulated in her head—or take a solitary breakfast while all those silent servants watched her?

'Only if you promise not to take any unnecessary risks.'

'Ah! So you *do* care?' he taunted.

'Only because if you're going to meet Leo, I'd like you to meet him in one piece.'

A sharp rap on the door put an end to any further talk and a robed servant led them through the corridors to the vast stable complex, which was situated on the eastern side of the palace.

The sun was already warm as two grooms led a pair of magnificent stallions out into the yard—one golden and one black. Erin thought they looked like textbook versions of equine perfection with their coats gleaming in the brightness of the morning light. In the far distance she could see the Sheikh making his way towards them, his usual phalanx of servants surrounding him. She noticed that he was wearing his robes, not jodhpurs—and wondered how on earth he could ride in them.

Dimitri moved towards the horses and she watched his every step, wishing she weren't so shockingly aware of his muscular body and the sun gilding his thick hair. She wasn't surprised to see him jump onto the golden horse, which seemed to echo his own colouring, but wondered why the two men briefly shook hands before the king mounted his own ebony stallion. For a few moments she watched as they trotted the horses round and round the yard. Dimitri was clearly trying to gauge the temperament of his mount and even a novice like Erin could see that the animal was powerful and strong. A flicker of apprehension ran down her spine. He'd given her all that spiel about having learned to ride in the Russian army and how brilliant the teaching had been, but he hadn't actually mentioned how long ago it was since he'd last ridden.

She could see the Sheikh leaning across to say something to him and the quick flash of anticipation in Dimitri's eyes made Erin stiffen. Because she knew that look. It was the same look he used to wear when poised on the brink of some monumental deal. The same look which usually heralded a long night spent drinking, or playing cards. It was a reckless look, edged with danger, and it took her right back to a place where she used to be frozen with fear, just wondering what the hell he was going to do next and imagining the worst.

She knew then that he had just accepted a challenge from the Sheikh—who just happened to be one of the world's most accomplished horsemen. *The stupid fool was going to race against a man with way more experience than himself.*

Her first thought was one of anger, because he'd told her he'd changed. He'd said he'd become Mr Respectable and she knew now why she'd found it so hard to believe. Because it wasn't true. Respectable men didn't race a temperamental thoroughbred they'd never ridden before, did they? They didn't take their life in their hands—especially when they hadn't even met the son they'd made so much fuss about meeting.

She wanted to dash over to stop them and she did actually take a step forward before sanity prevailed. Because what good could she do in a land where the king was hell-bent on racing a man desperate to buy some of his oil fields? Did she really think that either Dimitri or Saladin would listen to *her*?

She watched as they lined the two horses up at the edge of the gallops, sensing the excitement in the restless stallions as they strained forward. Suddenly, one of the servants fired a loud starting pistol but barely had Erin recovered from her startled reaction, when the two men took off at a furious pace.

Barely able to breathe, she watched as they galloped past, two gleaming streaks of ebony and gold—their hooves pounding the ground like thunder. The Sheikh was ahead by a margin which was gradually increasing and for a moment she thought that Dimitri was going to do the sensible thing and just let him win. But she hadn't factored in his highly competitive nature. She could see the determination on his face as he pressed his thighs hard into the animal's flanks and she could read the hungry tension in the Russian's body as he crouched over the horse and urged it forward.

He was coming up closer to the man ahead of him, and then closer still. He had almost caught up with the king of Jazratan as they rounded the bend but now both horses were going at a breakneck pace. *Please just let him be safe,* prayed Erin as waves of emotion too complex to comprehend twisted her heart and stomach into knots.

The two men were now almost neck and neck and Erin saw the Sheikh glance over at the Russian as he tightened his own reins. She could see the strain and exhilaration on both their faces as they urged their mounts on. She could see the servants at the finishing line trying to position themselves, crouching down in an attempt to visually work out what was going to be a photo finish.

But as they approached the line the Sheikh's horse reared up as if something had spooked it and to Erin's horror she saw Saladin slipping down the side of the horse, as if in slow motion.

For one heart-stopping moment she thought the king was about to disappear under the pounding hooves to certain death when Dimitri drew close to the frightened animal. Collision seemed inevitable and Erin froze as the Russian reached out, somehow anchoring Saladin to the ebony horse while grabbing the other reins and managing to bring both animals to a shaky halt. Her knees grew weak. She felt the rush of relief, which was quickly replaced by one of anxiety as she saw the look of pain which briefly distorted Dimitri's features as he held on to the Sheikh as if his life depended on it.

And then grooms, servants, bodyguards came running out from the yard towards the two men and all hell broke loose.

CHAPTER SEVEN

'I'VE NEVER SEEN anything so reckless. Or so… so…*stupid*,' said Erin, her voice trembling with rage and fear as she held a golden goblet to Dimitri's parched lips. 'Here. Drink this.'

From his prone position on the velvet divan, Dimitri winced. 'What's in it?'

'Nothing stronger than water. And it's good for you. Which I suppose means you don't want it.'

He winced a little as he shifted his position on the divan. 'Are you angry with me, Erin?'

'Too right I am.' Unwanted emotions were exploding like fireworks inside her and she gritted her teeth as she registered the ashen colour of his face. 'You could have *died* out there!'

'But I didn't.'

'That's not the point,' she said stubbornly.

They were back in the palace after an incident which had clearly rocked all the spectators and left everyone in the palace reeling as they considered how much worse it could have been, if Dimitri hadn't prevented Saladin from falling beneath the hooves of the galloping horse. But the Sheikh had emerged from the incident unscathed and it was Dimitri who was hurt. Dimitri who had winced with pain after the doctor had examined him and ordered a full-body X-ray. With Erin at his side he had been taken to the nearby hospital and given the all-clear, but the bruising was bad and he'd been told to take it easy.

Erin had stuck to his side like glue and accompanied him back to his suite and soon after their arrival Saladin had turned up, still in the same robes he'd worn while riding. His face and hair had been covered in fine dust and he had looked dark and very sombre—but his gratitude had been heartfelt as he'd thanked Dimitri.

'I owe you,' he had said in a low voice. 'I owe you my life. And that means that we are now as brothers. Do you realise that, my friend?' And then he had embraced the Russian with a powerful bear hug, which had made Dimitri wince again, before sweeping out, his retinue following closely behind.

'You told me that you didn't do that whole danger thing any more,' Erin accused as she held the goblet of water to Dimitri's lips and made him drink another mouthful. 'You said you were respectable these days. You made out like you were a changed man. That you didn't drink vodka any more—'

'Which I don't.'

'Or embrace danger just for the sake of it.'

'Which I don't.'

'Oh, really?' She glared at him. 'So what was that all about out there? How long since you've ridden?'

He shrugged. 'I don't remember.'

'So what made you think you could take on one of the most celebrated horsemen in the world and *win*?'

'I *did* win.'

Erin glared. 'Only because the Sheikh nearly fell.'

'Exactly.' Dimitri stretched his long legs in front of him and through his half-closed eyes he subjected her to a mocking stare. 'And if I hadn't stopped to assist him, then I would have won by a much greater margin. We both know that.'

'Why accept the challenge in the first place when anyone else would have defined it as reckless?'

'Because I wanted to,' he said flatly. 'And because I'm doing business with a powerful man who might have considered it a sign of weakness if I had refused, thus putting the deal in jeopardy.'

'Your business deals are more important than your life, are they, Dimitri?'

'They are important,' he said, his voice suddenly cooling. 'They are a quantifiable success, unlike most other things in life.'

There was a soft rap on the door and Erin walked across the room to answer it, frustration simmering away inside her. Who was it this time? Why couldn't they just leave him alone and let him recover?

She didn't know who she expected to find but she was surprised to see a robed woman standing on the threshold—maybe because this was the only other woman she'd seen since she'd arrived in Jazratan. Petite and slender and wearing a silvery veil, which provided the perfect backdrop for her lustrous ebony hair, she was holding a small pot in her hands. Rather surprisingly, her smile was confident and she didn't appear in the least bit shy.

'The Sheikh has sent me,' she said, in the loveliest accent Erin had ever heard. 'To minister to the esteemed Russian who today risked his life to save our beloved monarch.'

Erin's hackles started rising; she couldn't help herself. Was she imagining the gleam in the woman's doe-like eyes or the anticipatory curve of her soft smile as she looked over towards where

Dimitri lay on the divan? A whisper of apprehension washed over her skin. No, she was not.

'What do you mean, *"minister"*?' she questioned, more sharply than she had intended.

The woman's smile grew serene. 'This rare cream has many healing properties,' she said softly. 'It is made from the fire berries which grow in the foothills of the mountains to the far north of our country and after I have applied it the Sheikh's saviour will feel no more pain, and the bruising on his skin will disappear as if by magic.'

Erin wasn't sure if it was paranoia or just a powerful sense of something territorial, but she knew that *no way* was this gorgeous young creature going to start slapping cream all over Dimitri's chest. A thought occurred to her. It came out of nowhere but for some reason it stuck firmly in her mind and wouldn't seem to budge. Did Saladin realise that she and the Russian weren't having sex—had Dimitri told him that? And was he sending this luscious woman to Dimitri's suite as some primitive way of *thanking* him? Nothing would surprise her about an autocratic king like Saladin, who ruled a country where the opposite sex seemed almost invisible.

Coolly, she removed the pot from the woman's hands and smiled at her. 'Thank you so much for taking the time to bring this, and please convey our deepest gratitude to His Royal Highness,' she said. 'But I think Dimitri would prefer me to *minister* it.'

She closed the door in the woman's startled face and turned around to see the faintest glint of humour lighting Dimitri's eyes, before he winced again—as if it hurt to attempt to smile.

'You meant it, didn't you?' he said weakly as she began to walk across the room towards him. 'You're going to apply the cream yourself.'

'I did,' she said. 'And I am.'

'Be gentle with me, Erin.'

'Why wouldn't I be?'

'The look on your face does not suggest gentleness.'

Putting the fire-berry potion down on a table beside the divan, she began to unbutton his silky riding shirt, aware that it was clinging like damp tissue paper to the sweat-sheened muscles. She told herself that this was exactly the reason why she had gained a first-aid certificate and remembered the need to remain completely impartial. To treat him as she would treat anyone else requiring medical assistance. But the moment she began to massage the cream into the honed torso, she understood the challenge that impartiality presented. Dimitri's eyes were fully open now and there was a mocking light in their depths, as if they were asking a silent question which she didn't dare interpret—let alone answer.

Her fingers slid over his chest. It was sheer torture to touch him with this near-intimacy, even though she was doing her best to concentrate on the healing aspect and not on how delicious it felt to glide the cream over hard muscle covered by silky skin. But when he shifted his jodhpur-covered groin, it took all her determination not to be distracted by the distinct bulge there. Yet she couldn't look away, could she? She couldn't just stare at the wall. Instead, she focused intently on the bruises he had suffered and not the soft sigh which escaped from between his parted lips.

She continued to massage him, working intently and silently until she saw some of the tension leave his body. She put the pot down and went off to wash the cream from her hands but when she returned to the divan, she stared at his torso with a feeling of disbelief.

'Good grief,' she said faintly. 'Just look at that.'

Erin had spent years working for Dimitri, but she'd never seen that look of genuine astonishment on his face before, as he followed the direction of her gaze. And no wonder—for the bruises had reduced dramatically. The livid purple marks which had stained the golden skin had faded several shades lighter.

His eyes narrowed. 'What the hell happened? Did you wave a magic wand or something?'

She could see the flicker of a pulse at his temple. She saw the gleam of his torso and suddenly her throat grew dry. 'It must have been the potion,' she managed.

His gaze mocked her. 'Is that what it was?'

Erin stood there, knowing she ought to get the hell out of there while she still could, but something was keeping her rooted there—as if her feet had been superglued to the spot. Her heart began to pound. Was it the *magnificence* of touching his half-naked body after all this time, or just the memory of how it had felt when he was deep inside her? She shook her head slightly, trying to erase the image from her mind, only the image was stubbornly refusing to budge. She swallowed. 'Perhaps you need to rest now.'

'Perhaps I do.'

He stretched out on the divan, his body outlined against the rich velvet and brocade cushions, but she noticed that his eyes were only half closed. She could see the icy glint of blue from between the thick lashes and she felt as if he was observing her. Watching her. Waiting to see what she would do next. She knew she ought to turn and walk away from him. She knew a lot of things, but the thing she knew above everything else was that she wanted to kiss him. To lose herself in his arms and shudder with pleasure. And it wasn't going to happen. She swallowed. There was a whole stack of reasons why intimacy would be a bad thing, and none of those had changed. But she was still standing there, wasn't she? Standing there feeling conflicted while she dug her finger-nails into the palms of her hands and longed for what she knew she shouldn't have.

'Can I get you anything else?' she questioned stiffly.

He gave a slow, watchful smile. 'Like what?'

The tension shimmering between them was now so intense that Erin felt as if a single word or movement would shatter it, but his expression gave nothing away. He was a contradiction, she realised. He was stubborn and proud and angry with her for keeping Leo hidden from him, but he still wanted her. She could read it in the smoky smoulder of his blue eyes and the tension in his body. He wanted her, but he wasn't going to act on it. Instinct told her the next step was all down to her. That the ball was in her court. She had turned him down last night and his pride would not allow him to be turned down again. If she wanted him, then she was going to have to reach out to him. Still she hesitated, because wasn't this yet another way of Dimitri exercising his power over her?

'I think you've had enough rehydration and fire-berry potion for the time being, so I'll let you rest,' she said, even though the words felt as if they might strangle her.

But then he smiled again—and that smile changed everything. Something inside her snapped, like a piece of elastic which had been stretched too far, and suddenly she was doing what she'd only dreamed of doing in her most forbidden fantasies. She was leaning over him and brushing her lips over his—like a role reversal of the prince trying to waken the sleeping princess with his kiss.

Only, Dimitri was awake. Wide awake. The smile died on his lips. His calculating gaze lasted only a second before he hooked his hand behind her neck and brought her face back down to his.

She stared into his blue eyes. 'I...I shouldn't have done that.'

'Yes, you should,' he growled. 'And now you're going to do it all over again.'

He smelt of horse and dust and desire, underpinned with the faint scent of fire berries, and Erin trembled as he pulled her close and kissed her. She worried about her weight pushing against his battered body, but he didn't seem to care. He didn't seem to care about anything except deepening the kiss so that she quickly became weak with longing, but she drew her head back when she heard him moan.

'Am I hurting you?' she whispered.

'No.' Grabbing her ponytail as if it was a rope, he tipped her head back so that she was caught in the spotlight of his eyes. 'But I am at something of a disadvantage, since the doctor has suggested I avoid any strenuous movement.' His eyes gleamed. 'And since I am in no position to undress you or to master you—I think you will have to play the dominatrix this time.'

Erin froze. Until her sister had lent her *that* book last year, she hadn't even known what the word 'dominatrix' *meant*. She wondered if he was expecting some kind of souped-up sexual performance from her. Yet here was she—not a virgin, but very nearly. Did she come straight out and tell him that?

'You know,' he said, filling the silence, 'the suggestion wasn't supposed to make your eyes widen with horror. That is not what a man intends when he wants to have sex with a woman.'

'I don't want you to be disappointed.'

His hand still wrapped around her ponytail, he steered her face towards his. 'What are you talking about?'

'I'm not very…experienced.'

'Some men might consider a lack of experience to be a positive advantage.'

'And are you one of those men?'

He shook his head. 'Not now, Erin. I know how much you love to talk, but now is not a good time to discuss my sexual preferences.' His expression changed. 'Because every time you react to one of my remarks, you jerk your head back—causing your hips to slide over mine. And as a result, my erection is getting stronger by the minute—a fact which cannot have escaped you, *zvezda moya*.'

No, of course it hadn't escaped her. She didn't need to be experienced to realise just how aroused he was. She could feel the unfamiliar ridge pressing hard against one of her thighs and she told herself that now was the time for her to get off the divan and suggest putting more distance between them, not less. *Because surely that was what any sane person in her position would do.*

'We aren't supposed to be doing this,' she whispered as the finger which had been at the base of her neck began to slide slowly downwards.

'This?'

She forced herself to say it. To say it as it was and not how she'd like it to be. 'Sex.'

His finger stilled in its tantalising journey towards her breast. 'Do you want to stop?'

She closed her eyes, as if blotting out the distraction of his face could help her come to the right decision, but even that didn't help. She wriggled and shook her head. 'No,' she breathed.

'So stop analysing,' he instructed. 'And take off my clothes.'

Dimitri could feel her trembling as she unclipped the waistband of his jodhpurs and heard her unsteady rush of breath as she eased down the straining zipper. He shifted uncomfortably on the divan, trying to focus on something other than his body, trying to slow down the race of his own desire—because he could never remember sexual desire feeling quite so potent, nor so *dangerous*.

As she began to peel the jodhpurs down over his thighs he forced himself to remember that, for all her supposed sweetness and innocence, he couldn't trust her. He'd put Erin Turner in a different category from any other woman he'd ever known, and he was a fool to have done so. Because she wasn't different. She was exactly the same. Selfish. Calculating. Single-minded. She hadn't even given him a chance to get to know his son, or to see whether he'd changed, because it hadn't suited her to do so. *And because children were nothing but pawns in the lives of women.* How could he have forgotten a truth as fundamental as that?

His anger had made him even more aroused—something he hadn't thought possible—and he enjoyed the darkening of her eyes as he breathed out a series of instructions to her. 'Go over to my wash bag and find my condoms. No, let me put it on—you just concentrate on taking off your dress. Mmm… That's better. Now your panties. And your bra. And then climb on top of me and take me inside you. *Da.* Just like that. Oh, God, Erin—just like that.'

With his hands on her narrow hips and her small breasts positioned perfectly for his delectation, he watched as she came very quickly. And so did he. Too quickly, perhaps. He could have carried on having sex with her for hours and already his desire was returning with an intensity which took his breath away, but he forced himself to roll to the other side of the large divan— as if putting distance between them was the only sensible thing he'd done all day.

'What did you mean?' he asked, when eventually his breathing was steady enough for him to make himself understood. 'When you said you weren't very experienced?'

Her eyes were wary as she looked at him—like a small animal who had inadvertently wandered into a hostile domain—and she shrugged, as if embarrassed.

'It doesn't matter.'

'It does,' he contradicted.

'Because you say so?'

He smiled. 'Precisely.'

She began to play with the ends of her hair. 'You're the only man I've ever had sex with.'

A sudden silence fell between them. Her answer was so unexpected that it took a moment for him to process it.

'Why?' he said, at last.

'Why do you think?' Her words came out in a rush, as if she had been bottling them up for a long time. 'First I was pregnant and then I had a tiny baby who wasn't very fond of sleeping, which meant I kept dozing off at various points during the day and forgetting to wash my hair and my tops always seemed to be stained with milk. That's never really a good look. And then the baby grew into a demanding toddler who was into everything, so that I felt like some kind of maternal health and safety expert trying to keep him out of trouble. I was helping my sister with the café and trying to keep our heads above water and I...' Her words faded away and a shuttered look came over her face, as if she'd said too much and only just realised it. 'There was never really time for men.'

'So if I was your first lover—'

'You *knew* that?'

He gave a faint smile. 'Of course I knew it. I may have often been accused of a lack of sensitivity towards women—but never when it comes to sex.'

Her green eyes looked confused. 'But you didn't...you didn't mention it at the time.'

'And neither did you.' He shrugged. 'That night was supposed to be about pleasure—not an anatomical discussion about why your hymen was still intact.'

Her green eyes spat fire as she pulled the coverlet up over her breasts. 'How *callous* you can be, Dimitri!'

'You think so?' He narrowed his eyes as he looked at her. 'Don't you think that after everything which has happened between us, we now deserve the truth?'

'Even if the truth hurts?'

'But being hurt is a part of life. A big part of it—as is regret,' he said. 'And if you must know, I was angry with myself for having sex with you that night.'

'Angry?' She sounded bewildered. 'Why?'

'Because you were an employee and I liked you that way. I had crossed a line I never intended to cross. And because it is a responsibility when a man takes a woman's virginity.'

'Responsibility?' She repeated the word in horror.

'Of course it is,' he said. 'I didn't want you fixating on me, or clinging to me or deciding that I was the man who was going to make you happy. And I just couldn't work out how it had happened, that was the most frustrating thing. How years of a perfectly satisfying platonic relationship had suddenly erupted into something which was so unbelievably X-rated. So tell me, Erin—since we're being truthful—did you choose me because you were aware of my reputation as a lover and considered me the most suitable candidate to take your virginity? Because you knew that I was the man most likely to give you pleasure?'

She didn't answer straight away and when she did, her voice was shaking. 'You flatter yourself,' she said. 'As well as misjudging me, if you think I could have been that cold-blooded about it. I didn't *choose* you. It just happened.'

'You just *happened* to bring a totally unnecessary batch of paperwork round to my apartment when it could have waited until morning?'

'I was worried about you,' she said. 'Worried sick, if you must know. You seemed to have a permanent hangover and to exist on no sleep. Your bodyguard told me you were living like a vampire. And then he resigned and there was all that trouble in Paris and I didn't trust your new bodyguard one bit. Every time the phone rang I thought it was going to be the hospital telling me you'd been admitted. Or the morgue telling me you were lying on a slab…'

'So you thought a little creature comfort might

bring me to my senses?' he mocked as her words tailed off. 'That a taste of the pure and innocent Erin Turner might be enough to make me see the error of my ways?'

'You are hateful, Dimitri.'

'Maybe I am. But I've never pretended to be anything else,' he said, steeling himself against the hurt which was clouding her green eyes and telling himself it was better this way. Because although she'd told him she didn't believe in love, he wasn't sure he believed her. Women were programmed to believe in it, weren't they? Better she didn't start thinking he was someone who was capable of providing her with happiness. Especially not domestic happiness. 'Didn't anyone ever teach you that it's a bad idea to go to a man's apartment late at night, looking so unbelievably sexy?'

'I was wearing my navy work suit and a white shirt!' she protested. 'It was hardly what you'd call provocative.'

'Not intentionally, no.' His voice deepened.

'But you were. I'll never forget the sight of you standing there, all wide-eyed and soaking wet.'

'I didn't know it was going to rain!'

'And I wasn't expecting my secretary to ring the doorbell looking as if she'd just taken part in a wet T-shirt competition.'

He hadn't been planning to kiss her, either. It had been a combination of factors which had made something inside him snap. Her wide-eyed look of concern, which had contrasted with the erotic spectacle of that forbidding suit clinging to her slim body. Her complete obliviousness as to how *sexy* she looked had sealed her fate. He had been existing in such a dark place for so long and in that moment Erin had looked like a beacon of light. He'd given in to impulse and kissed her. And hadn't the way she'd responded driven him wild? He remembered being taken aback that his unassuming secretary should suddenly morph into a little wildcat when he'd taken her in his arms. He remembered telling himself he

would stop. Just one more kiss and he would definitely stop…

But he hadn't stopped, had he? He had been
unable to prevent himself from plunging into
her tight, wet warmth and being the first man
ever to possess her. He remembered that he had
never come quite so many times in one night.
That he seemed to have a permanent hard-on
whenever he looked at her. Yet his conscience
had troubled him afterwards and *that* in itself
was unusual, for he had been brought up to believe that conscience was a waste of time. Had he
known on some subliminal level before he'd even
kissed her that she was innocent—and didn't that
make his subsequent self-contempt seem a little
hypocritical?

The only honourable thing he'd done was to
make sure he'd used contraception—even if it
had subsequently failed. And then he had left
the country.

Had he been afraid that desire would overcome
him again? That he would become one of those

clichéd men who slept with their secretary and she'd end up knowing everything about him, instead of just the lion's share? Or was he just afraid that he would hurt her very badly—and someone like Erin did not deserve to be hurt.

But it seemed that he had been regarding her through rose-tinted spectacles and that she had been perfectly capable of her own brand of deception and lies. Her own brand of hurt.

An uneasy silence had fallen again and he didn't object when she climbed off the divan and bent down to pick up her discarded clothes. He felt more in control when she was away from him and control was vital. Especially now. Because nothing had changed, he reminded himself grimly. She had kept their son hidden from him. She was no friend to him.

The armful of clothes was concealing her naked breasts, but her neck was flushed pink and the dark triangle of hair at the fork of her thighs made his body flood with another powerful wave of lust.

And it wasn't going to happen, he told himself grimly. *There was going to be no more intimacy, no matter how much he wanted it. Because sex with Erin Turner didn't feel anonymous—it made him feel exposed and weak. And he didn't do weak.*

'So what do you think we should do now?' she questioned, her voice breaking into his uncomfortable thoughts.

'Now?' He could hear the uncertainty in her voice and it pleased him. It made him feel in control again—even if he had to shift his body beneath the coverlet to hide his growing erection. 'I shall rest for a while as the doctor instructed—and after that I shall meet with the Sheikh, as was originally planned. I'm sure you can find plenty with which to amuse yourself in the meantime. There is a magnificent library here in the palace, or you could ask one of the

servants to show you around the gardens. I believe they are very famous.' He let his heavy eyelids fall and failed to stifle a yawn as he blotted
out the unsettling look of distress in her eyes.
'But I am weary now, Erin—so let me sleep.'

CHAPTER EIGHT

HOW *COULD* SHE?

Erin walked to the edge of the man-made lake which dominated the sheltered grounds at the rear of the palace and stared gloomily at the gleaming water. How could she have done something so fundamentally *self-destructive*? She'd had sex with Dimitri. Despite knowing that it was the action of a fool, she had walked straight into it.

The sun dazzled off the glittering surface of the lake and now and then an exotic bird would swoop down to drink. These gardens were like an oasis—one of the most beautiful places she'd ever visited—yet all Erin could think about was that erotic episode on the divan yesterday, following Dimitri's riding accident.

He'd been so matter-of-fact about it afterwards,

displaying a cold-bloodedness she remembered from watching him doing countless business deals. Once that amazing bout of sex was over, he seemed to have retreated from her—physically *and* mentally—just like last time. He hadn't touched her again, had just rolled over and turned his back on her and gone to sleep. And even though she'd told herself that his body was still recovering from the accident on the horse—it had only increased her feelings of mortification.

She had gone back to her own suite, feeling empty and a little bit *cheap*, and the long shower she'd taken afterwards hadn't made her feel much better. But she had done her best to stay calm and tried very hard to keep herself occupied, because activity stopped her brooding and dwelling on what she'd done. She explored the palace library as Dimitri had suggested and made it her personal mission to find her way around the bewildering maze of wide marble corridors which made up the Al Mektala residence. She spent several hours being driven out into the desert—

accompanied by the woman who had brought the fire-berry lotion to Dimitri's suite, who actually turned out to be very sweet. And although she had tried to take in the stark beauty of the stark desert sands, unwanted images of Dimitri's ice-blue eyes kept flashing through her mind.

And he hadn't come near her. He hadn't touched her, or kissed her. There had been no silent message which had passed between them to acknowledge their shared intimacy.

Erin kept trying to convince herself that this new stand-off was sensible. More sex would complicate an already complicated situation—she *knew* that. Yet she was finding his behaviour more wounding than any open hostility. He was treating her with all the polite indifference he might have shown to a passing waitress at a cocktail party. As if the man who had kissed her so passionately yesterday morning was nothing but a figment of her imagination. She found herself dressing for their final dinner at the palace with a heavy heart.

When he knocked, she opened the door to find him wearing a darker than usual suit, which made him look powerful and forbidding.

'I'm having a final meeting with Saladin before dinner, so I'll come back and collect you once it's over,' he said, his hair gleaming molten gold beneath the glittering chandelier. 'Oh, and we will leave for London tomorrow. The jet will be ready for us in the morning. I'm sure you'll be keen to get back.'

'Absolutely.' Erin was determined to match his cool demeanour even though her teeth were gritted behind her smile. 'I'll ring my sister.'

'You spoke to her earlier?'

'Yes.'

'How's Leo?' he asked suddenly.

'He's fine.'

There was a pause. 'He hasn't missed you too much?'

'It's barely been two days.' She hesitated, because this was the closest they'd come to conversation since they'd had sex and she found herself wanting to prolong it. To pretend that everything was normal when nothing felt normal. 'Has the Sheikh come to any decision about selling you the oil fields?'

He finished knotting his tie—a blue silk affair one shade darker than his eyes. 'He says he'll give me his answer this evening. Though I suspect that is simply a formality and his answer will be yes.'

'You sound surprised.'

'I suppose I am—a little. After all these years of one step forward, two steps back—the deal has been much more straightforward than I ever anticipated.'

'Because you saved his life?'

He shrugged. 'Probably.'

She shifted from one foot to the other, aware that her composure was in danger of deserting her as the reality of returning to London loomed before her. 'What's going to happen when we get back?'

He lifted his dark brows in query. 'In regard to?'

Her heart began to pound. 'Leo, of course. About you…getting to know him.'

He raised his eyebrows. 'You would prefer it if I didn't?'

To Erin's horror his words struck a chord, highlighting a part of herself she didn't like. A selfish, horrible part which made her wish he would just disappear and take with him his ability to inflict pain and hurt on her stupidly vulnerable heart. 'No,' she said, wondering if he could hear the hesitation in her voice. 'That isn't what I want, but…'

'But? You still think I'm unsuitable? I've failed the Erin Turner fit-to-be-a-father test? You think I'll be dragging him to the nearest bar or casino as soon as he's old enough?'

She met the challenge in his eyes, reminding herself that her own feelings weren't the issue here—but those of her son were paramount. And Dimitri needed to know that. He needed to know that she would fight with everything she possessed to protect her little boy from being hurt or disappointed.

'No, I don't think that,' she said. 'You don't seem like that kind of man any more. But there are other considerations, Dimitri.'

'To do with you?'

She shook her head. Did he think she was about to start clinging to him because they'd just had sex? 'No. To do with him. I don't want you coming into his life on a whim. You can't just waltz in and tell him you're his father and decide you don't really like fatherhood—before disappearing again.'

'So what are you suggesting?'

'I'm just asking you to give it a little time before you tell him who you are. In case you want to walk away. I'm giving you an opt-out clause in case you change your mind.' She held up her hand, as if anticipating his objections. 'Because children take up a lot of time. They're demanding. They need love and reassurance and stability—and it's constant. You can't just close the door on them and tell them to go away. You've always lived life on your terms, Dimitri—more than anyone else I've ever known. You might find the responsibilities of parenthood don't suit you, and if that's the case, then that's fine. No one is going to condemn you for that—least of all me. I just don't want you making promises to him. Promises you are unable to keep. Surely you can understand that?'

Their gazes clashed for a moment before he nodded his head.

'Yes, I can understand,' he said as he left her suite and headed towards the Sheikh's private apartments, thinking about everything she'd said and the painful honesty with which she'd chosen her words. He was beginning to understand now that when it came to Leo, she was the one with all the power and it was rare for him to be in the weaker position. Was that why he had stayed away from her since the erotic encounter after his riding accident—because that was *his* way of wielding power? He had known that he could have taken her in his arms at any time and had her gasping with desire within minutes. But something had stopped him.

What was it? Something to do with the way she made him feel? As if he were some sort of jig-saw which had been scattered and she was eager to put all the pieces back together again. And he didn't want that. He didn't want anyone *recon-structing* him.

The corridors were cool as he walked towards the Sheikh's private apartments and he could see the outline of the moon beginning to appear in the still blue sky. He thought how ironic it was that for months this had been the one thing he'd wanted above all else. A deal with Saladin Al Mektala. Oil in exchange for diamonds. A foothold in the Middle East at last and a triumph to eclipse all his most recent triumphs.

But suddenly its allure seemed to have faded and all he could think about was the little boy with the golden hair and eyes so like his own. And inevitably those thoughts led back to Erin…

He was shown into a high-ceilinged room which resembled a cross between a library and a study. Oil paintings of magnificent horses lined the walls and priceless artefacts drew the eye like museum pieces. On the Sheikh's desk was a photo of Saladin holding the prestigious Omar Cup, a gleaming chestnut stallion beside him, and Dimitri took a moment to study it.

'That was one of my proudest moments,' said Saladin, his deep voice breaking the silence as he emerged from the shadows of the room, his eyes following the direction of the Russian's gaze.

'But?' said Dimitri, lifting his gaze from the photo and supplying the word which seemed to hang in the air, like the rich incense which scented the room.

The Sheikh's eyes gleamed as he sat down behind the desk and indicated a chair opposite for Dimitri.

'Victory seems irrelevant when you are forced to face your own mortality as I have had to do,' he said heavily. 'If it had been another man but you

racing against me, I might not be here today—
for the desert lands breed many enemies who
would have been glad to see me disfigured, or to
have perished. Who would have enjoyed seeing
me fall beneath all the galloping power of those
two mighty horses, knowing that I have no living heir and that all my lands would pass into
the hands of a distant branch of the family.' The
king's black eyes gleamed. 'But then, few men
other than you would have accepted my challenge
to race, for all kinds of reasons.'

'But how could I resist a challenge from a
king?' said Dimitri mockingly.

'Even if doing so caused obvious distress to the
beautiful woman accompanying you?'

For some reason it irritated Dimitri to hear
Saladin describe Erin as beautiful. He had not
brought her here to be gazed at and compli-
mented by a powerful sheikh. 'I do not live my
life in accordance with the wishes of others,' he
said stiffly. 'I act as I see fit.'

'But your actions placed you in mortal danger.'

Dimitri shrugged. 'To brush with death is inevitable. It is part of life itself.'

Saladin picked up a gleaming golden pen. 'But the timing of such a brush is crucial, don't you think? And this one especially so. It has made me re-examine my life. I wonder if it will make you do the same.' Abruptly, he signed the thick sheet of parchment which lay before him and then looked up. 'The oil fields are yours.'

Dimitri inclined his head. 'Thank you.'

'My lawyers will be in touch. But, Dimitri—'

Dimitri had been about to rise from the chair until the monarch's unfamiliar use of his first name made him pause.

He raised his eyebrows. 'Majesty?'

The Sheikh paused, as if he was about to start speaking in a language unfamiliar to him. 'I recognise in you someone with demons,' he said softly. 'The demons which seem to plague all successful men. And sometimes the only way to rid ourselves of them is to confront them without fear.'

The Sheikh's words echoed around his head as Dimitri made his way back to his suite. It was a curiously personal remark for a king to make—especially one with the stony reputation of Saladin. Was the bond forged between them over that near-fatal race responsible for such an uncharacteristic statement, and was it true? Dimitri shut the door behind him. *Were* his demons still dominating his life because he had failed to reach out and confront them?

He realised that it was not just Erin's deception which had angered him, or the powerlessness he'd felt about being presented with a fatherhood he had not chosen. It was the fear of fatherhood itself. Would his inability to love or nurture damage that laughing little boy whose life was materially poor but emotionally rich? And Saladin's words came back to him again. Surely he had to *try*.

He went to Erin's suite to take her to dinner and she looked up from the book she was reading. The gleam of the chandeliers shone on her dark hair and the claret silk dress caressed her slender body, and automatically he felt his body stiffen with desire. But desire could cloud your judgement. It could distract you from the things which really mattered—and right now he knew what mattered most.

He stared into Erin's green eyes, knowing how incompatible their two lifestyles were. He hadn't known precisely what it was he wanted, or how he was going to go about the daunting task of discovering fatherhood.

Until now.

The idea hit him with a sudden resolve. A primitive and bone-deep certainty, which seemed to have been inspired by Saladin's words. It felt like a distant call to his own ancestry—yet how could that make any sense when his past was so tainted and warped?

But sometimes instinct could be stronger than reason and there was no waver in his voice as he spoke. 'I want to take Leo to my country,' he said.

The book slipped from her fingers.

'You mean, to Russia?'

Something stirred deep within his heart as he nodded.

'*Da*. To Russia,' he echoed, and saw the uncertainty which clouded her face.

CHAPTER NINE

A DISTANT DOOR slammed and a little boy came running into the room, pulling off his waterproof jacket and shaking his head like a puppy. Raindrops showered down over the worn carpet as Erin stepped forward to take the jacket from her son.

'Hello, darling,' she said, trying to act as normally as possible, but it wasn't easy. How could she act normally when Dimitri was standing there staring at Leo—his blue eyes burning with what looked like a distinct sense of ownership? She thought how out of place he looked in his expensive grey suit, dominating the small room at the back of the café. She wished she'd asked her sister to stay for some moral support, but had decided against it at the last minute. She needed to do this on her own. With Leo. Just the three of them. Swallowing down her anxiety, she replaced it with a bright smile as she looked at her son. 'Darling, I want you to meet a friend of mine.'

Leo, a child who always seemed to be in perpetual motion, stood and stared up at the man with all the unembarrassed curiosity of a child.

'What's your name?'

'Dimitri. And you're Leo.'

'Who told you that?'

'Your mummy did.'

A silent look passed between them.

'Why do you talk in that funny voice?'

'Because I am from Russia.'

'Where's Russia?'

Dimitri smiled. 'It is a vast and magnificent land which straddles both Europe and Asia. We have lots of snow in winter and very beautiful buildings which are like no others you will ever see. I could show you where it is on a map if you would like that.' He lifted his gaze to Erin's. 'Do you have any maps around the place, Erin?'

'I'm sure I can find one,' she said, but her heart was beating very fast and she wasn't sure why.

It turned out to be one of the most bizarre evenings of her life. During occasional moments of wistfulness or vulnerability, she'd sometimes tried to picture Dimitri with his son but had found it impossible to imagine the icy oligarch being warm and loving towards a child. Maybe she had misjudged him, or he was a better actor than she'd thought—because soon Leo was sitting happily up beside him as he pointed out seas and rivers on the map.

She'd told him that he couldn't just swoop into their lives and carry Leo off to Russia—that he had to get to know the little boy first. She just hadn't expected it to go so *well*. And when, a week later, she walked into the room and found two heads of molten gold bent over the table together in silent concentration as Dimitri showed Leo a photograph, a shiver of something like fear whispered over her skin.

Already they were sharing secrets.

Already she was the outsider.

'What's that?' she said, glancing down at the photograph, which showed a beautiful house.

Dimitri raised his head. 'It's a place outside Moscow which I own.'

'That's…nice,' she said, her voice growing uncertain.

He smiled but Erin could see a flicker of triumph in his blue eyes. 'And I think we should take Leo there,' he said.

'Can we go, Mummy?' Leo was asking, a look of excitement on his face. '*Can* we?'

Erin stared into the eyes which glittered so icily above Leo's head and felt a punch of helpless rage. Hadn't he ever heard of consensus? Of running it past her first? Of course not. He didn't negotiate with women, because they always caved in and gave him exactly what he wanted. 'I'm not sure if I can get anyone to cover for me at the café—not at such short notice.'

'I can get you all the cover you need,' he said,

with cool assurance. 'Neither you nor your sister need worry about a thing.'

He was just going to throw money at the problem, Erin thought. And there was nothing she could do to stop it. This was going to happen whether she liked it or not.

'In that case, I don't see why not,' she said lightly. 'It's half-term next week, after all.'

Moscow was a city straight out of a fairy tale. As if Walt Disney had met with the local architects and been given a free hand in its design. Intricate buildings were topped with brightly coloured turrets shaped like artichokes. Golden monuments dazzled with giant stars. Statuesque government buildings lined the wide Moskva River, where boats drifted by in slow motion—all seen from the helicopter which had been waiting to whisk them away from the airport.

Despite her reservations about the trip, Erin could feel a growing sense of excitement as she looked around, while Leo was almost incoherent with delight as the bird-like craft whirred over the Russian capital.

'Will it snow?' asked Leo eagerly as he stared up into the clear blue sky. 'Will it? My teacher says it always snows in Russia.'

'Not always,' answered Dimitri. 'It usually starts at the end of October, so we may just miss it.'

Leo scowled. 'But I want snow. I want to build a snowman!'

'In that case…' Dimitri smiled '…we might just have to come back again when it's colder.'

His words made Erin's fingers stiffen as she wound her new pashmina around her neck. She was trying not to fret about how her son would readjust to life in Bow after a trip like this, because how could he fail to be affected by Dimitri's lifestyle? If he'd tasted private jets and helicopters and fast cars, surely it would seem mundane to have to hop on the local bus. If the man organising all this had only to lift his hand for someone to cater to his every whim—as had been demonstrated on every step of their journey—then wouldn't Leo be seduced by that, no matter how hard she'd tried to bring him up to appreciate the simple things in life?

And what about her? Was she also in danger of being affected by the Russian influence and undeniable sex appeal? She'd been so sure of the person she was. Someone who didn't want to believe in love any more. Someone who'd had her fingers burned and her heart bruised when she'd fallen for her oligarch boss all those years ago. She'd convinced herself that she had learned her lesson and would never allow herself to feel like that again.

So why was Dimitri dominating her thoughts like a pop song she couldn't get out of her head? She knew he was no good for her. He'd made it clear he no longer wanted her. He'd had sex with her and then just pushed her away afterwards. He'd rejected her all over again and it hurt. It hurt like hell.

She shot a glance at his profile, at the high

slash of his cheekbones and hard set of his lips. The sun was flooding into the helicopter, making him look precious and powerful—as if he'd been dipped in gold.

'Look down there,' said Dimitri, his rich accent breaking into her troubled thoughts. 'We're nearly there.'

They were passing over a huge patch of dark and impenetrable trees before beginning their descent towards the smooth circle of a helipad on the outskirts of the forest. A rush of air came up to meet them and a man on the ground signalled to the pilot—his hair plastered to his head as the craft came rocking to a halt. The blades stopped spinning and Dimitri jumped out, holding up his arms to Leo, while Erin exited the craft with as much grace as possible, glad she'd worn trousers.

A four-wheel drive was waiting and Dimitri took the wheel, speeding along a straight road which looked uncannily quiet after the crowded streets of Moscow. Soon they were entering the forest through a concealed and guarded entrance and passing mansion after mansion, some completely hidden behind high, dense hedges, while others offered a tantalising glimpse of turrets and towers.

Dimitri indicated left and the car swung through a huge pair of electronic gates and Erin peered out of the window. 'What is this place?' she asked.

'It's a private estate and each house is called a *dacha*. In England some people own second homes in the country and this is similar. Many Russians have them. It's where I did most of my growing up.'

'I thought you grew up in Moscow.'

'No. My father was in the city a lot, but my mother preferred it here. They call it Moscow's secret city. Many people think it doesn't exist—that it's just a myth—but as you can see for yourself, it isn't. Just that not everyone knows where to find it, and that's deliberate. It's where the rich live—and play. Where there's no pressure to be modest and no shame in showing off your wealth. They say that security here is tighter than in the Kremlin and very few outsiders are permitted entry. You should count yourself privileged, Erin.'

Privileged? She felt closer to panic, especially when Leo clutched at her hand.

'Look, Mummy—look!'

Erin turned her head to see him pointing towards a stunning art deco house, which Erin recognised immediately. It was the house from the photograph. Up close, the tall house was even larger and more imposing than it had appeared in the glossy photo, and the unusual curved wooden door made it look like something out of a fairy tale.

There were so many questions Erin wanted to ask but there wasn't time because the front door was being opened by a homely-looking woman whose creased face broke into a wide smile when she saw Dimitri. She looked as if she wanted to fling her arms around him but didn't quite dare. And Erin was surprised by one of the most unguarded smiles she'd ever seen on the oligarch's face as he bent his head to kiss the woman's cheeks before speaking to her in rapid Russian.

'This is Svetlana,' he said, 'who used to look after me when I was a little boy, even younger than you are now, Leo. Svetlana—this is Erin, Leo's mother.'

'You are very…welcome,' said Svetlana in halting English, her eyes softening as she looked down at Leo. 'Come inside, little one. You must be tired.'

Automatically, Leo shook his head. 'I'm not tired,' he said.

'Well, that is good!' Svetlana smiled. 'I wonder, do you like gingerbread, Leo? We have much famous gingerbread here in Russia and we like to eat it with hot, sweet tea. It was Dimitri's favourite when he was a little boy. Would you like to try some?'

Expecting continued resistance, Erin glanced down at her son—but he was wearing the same expression he'd had the first time she'd taken him to meet Father Christmas. Was the child who was notoriously picky when it came to food really taking Svetlana's outstretched hand and wandering off with her towards the back of the house as if they'd known each other all their lives? It seemed he was.

For a while she stood listening to the sound of their retreating footsteps until at last they became silent and she was left alone with Dimitri. His hands were on her shoulders as he helped her out of her coat, his fingers brushing softly across her back and making her spine tingle.

'Come with me,' he said and she followed him into a reception room which overlooked the sweeping gardens at the back of the house. It was a breathtakingly impressive room and she looked around it with an undeniable sense of wonder. Who would ever have guessed that such an exquisite place lay in the middle of some random forest?

Fabergé eggs stood on gilded furniture, and a bonsai tree which stood in pride of place on a lacquered Chinese table made her think of his apartment in London. She walked over and stared at the perfectly formed miniature leaves and wondered how on earth he could get experts to come and tend it—all these miles from Moscow. How many apartments and houses and bonsai trees did he actually own? Did they all merge into one, she wondered—so that sometimes he forgot which city he was in? Were the women who passed through his life just as interchangeable as his houses?

She looked up to meet the blue ice of his gaze. 'Is this your real home?'

He gave an oblique smile. 'I visit here maybe three or four times a year—more if the opportunity arises.'

'You maintain a house this size just for the occasional visit?' She looked at him incredulously. 'Why would you do that?'

'Why not? Russians like owning bricks and mortar because they represent security. It is also Svetlana's home,' he added. 'And I owe her a debt of care. Her son tends the gardens here and his wife helps maintain the house.' His gaze drifted over her and lingered on her face. 'But my property empire isn't what's uppermost on my mind at the moment.'

His voice had deepened. It seemed to whisper over her skin like velvet, but she kept her voice careless. *He's not going to play games with you,* she thought fiercely. *He's just not.* 'Oh?'

His gaze was very steady. 'You may have noticed that I have been a little *cool* towards you.'

She tried not to react. 'Yeah, I've noticed.'

'And you're probably wondering why.'

'Don't worry, Dimitri—I'm not losing any sleep over it.'

He studied the bonsai tree for a moment, before glancing up again. 'I thought it would be better for both of us—and for Leo—if we attempted to keep our relationship platonic. I thought that what happened in Jazratan would be better kept as a one-off. I thought the fewer complications, the better. But maybe I was wrong.'

'Dimitri Makarov wrong?' she questioned sarcastically. 'Gosh. Can I have that in writing?'

'Because despite everything that has happened,' he continued, as if she hadn't spoken, 'and despite the note of caution in my head, there is one factor which outweighs all the others… and that is that I still want you, *zvezda moya*. In fact, I cannot believe how badly I want you.' He smiled. 'And I know enough about women to realise that the feeling is mutual.'

Erin met his eyes, trying to ignore the instinctive rush of heat to her body and to concentrate instead on his arrogant words. *Note of caution?* Had he really said that? Of course he had. Because not only was arrogance one of his faults—he also had a complete inability to recognise it! She drew in a shaky breath. 'Oh, I might want you,' she agreed. 'I'm not enough of a hypocrite to deny that.'

'So?' he questioned, unabashed, the hint of that smile still playing at the edges of his mouth.

Expectation was coming off him in waves

which were almost tangible and Erin felt a flare of anger. She recognised that there was an element of negotiation in what he was saying, but it wasn't enough. Not nearly enough. Was she expected to grab at whatever scraps he threw her? To settle for something which sounded like a reluctant afterthought?

'So, nothing! Do you really expect me to accommodate your see-sawing desires just like that?' she demanded, snapping her fingers in the air. 'To behave like an obedient puppet, just waiting for you to pull my strings one minute and then smilingly accept it when you put me back in the box the next?'

His eyes narrowed. 'Why the hell do you have to analyse everything to death?' he gritted.

'Because that's what women do,' she retorted. 'And we file it under self-respect. I may have made mistakes in the past and perhaps I should have acknowledged them sooner, but I'm doing my best to make amends for that now. I'm sorry I excluded you from Leo's life without giving you the opportunity to prove you've changed. That's one of the reasons I've come to Russia with you, even though it's…*difficult*. But there's no way I'm going to be treated like a convenient plaything while I'm here, no matter how many of my buttons you press. So if you'd please show me my room, I'd like to go and unpack.'

His face was a picture, Erin thought. A mixture of disbelief and fury as he muttered something decidedly angry in Russian before turning away and stomping towards the grand staircase. But his discomfiture was small consolation for the aching in her body and the even greater aching in her heart.

CHAPTER TEN

It was the first time in a long time that Erin had been given a room she could call her own. She'd shared a cramped bedroom with Leo since the day she'd first brought him home from hospital and was used to tiptoeing around and condensing her stuff into the smallest possible space while fighting a losing battle against clutter. But Leo was now ensconced in his own cosy set of rooms just along the corridor and playing with every remaining toy from Dimitri's childhood, which had been dragged down from the attic by Svetlana's son.

Following her explosive row with Dimitri, he had taken himself off to his study and shut the door very firmly behind him. It had been left to Svetlana to take her and Leo on a guided tour of the house, showing them the countless rooms, the beautiful gardens and finally the indoor swimming pool, which gleamed invitingly and made Leo squeal with delight. Erin felt her heart plummet. She hated swimming at the best of times and was dreading her son's next inevitable demand, when Dimitri walked into the pool complex.

'Do you like swimming, Leo?'

Erin's heart pounded as she looked up to meet the cool blue gaze, but there was no mockery or flirtation there. The briefest of smiles and a cursory nod were his only acknowledgement to her, before he crouched down to his son's level.

'He doesn't swim,' she said quickly.

'In that case, I can teach him.'

She didn't even get a chance to say that Leo had brought nothing suitable to wear in the water, because it seemed that swimming trunks and armbands were readily available and had already been purchased from a nearby department store. It made Erin realise that, behind the scenes, Dimitri must have been making plans for his son's arrival before she'd even agreed to the trip and that made her feel odd. Manipulated, almost. But she didn't have the heart to spoil Leo's fun and her guilty secret was that she enjoyed watching Dimitri put himself out for someone else in a way she'd never seen him do before. And wasn't the shameful truth that she also enjoyed looking at that powerful body in a pair of clinging swim-shorts, despite her intention to avert her gaze whenever he levered himself out of the water?

Water highlighted his masculinity. It gleamed and highlighted the golden skin and emphasised the honed contours of his powerful physique. It made her body sizzle with desire and she couldn't work out a way to stop it. And the most infuriating thing was that she could have had him. She could have had him on her first night here, and yet she had turned him down.

By the third day, Leo was not only becoming confident in the water—he was behaving as if he'd spent his whole life living in a luxurious *dacha*. He listened to Dimitri's firm house rules and obeyed them. He knew that the swimming pool was out of bounds unless there was an adult present and in the meantime he made friends with Svetlana's grandson, Anatoly—who was a year older. Erin watched from the sidelines, aware that there was a lot of Dimitri in her son which she'd never seen before. Or never *allowed* herself to see. With the large grounds at his disposal, a playmate and a football, he was able to enjoy the kind of healthy freedom which wasn't readily available in London.

She told herself she was grateful to Dimitri for his hospitality, but his polite and non-committal behaviour towards her was starting to drive her insane. Yet this was what she had actually *asked* for, so she was hardly in a position to complain about it. Was it simply a case of wanting what she couldn't have? Like when you tried to cut down on sugar and it left you craving something sweet.

Dimitri wasn't sweet. He was the antithesis of sweet. He was hard and strong and ruthless. But here he was showing a side of himself she'd never seen before. She'd never imagined he could be so *gentle*, or that his cold face could warm into such a breathtaking smile when he interacted with his little boy.

Suddenly, she felt like someone who had been left out in the cold. As if *she* were the outsider.

After dinner on the third night she'd gone to her room and shut the door behind her with a heavy sigh. She should have felt, if not exactly happy, then at least *content*. It had been another successful day. Dimitri had taken them deep into the forest in the crisp cold, and they'd all been worn out with fresh air and exercise. Leo was fast asleep next door and, although supper had been civilised and delicious, Dimitri had been called to the telephone soon afterwards and had excused himself. He had shut himself in his study and showed no sign of coming out and so Erin had come upstairs to bed.

She began to unbutton her cardigan, wondering how he would react if she went and found him and told him she'd changed her mind. That she no longer cared about being treated like a play-thing if only he would kiss her again. She hung the cardigan over the back of the chair and pulled a face at her washed-out reflection in the mirror. But that would be the action of an idiot, wouldn't it? Long-term pain for short-term gain.

She'd just put on her nightdress when there was a knock at the door and, thinking it might be Leo, she sped over to answer it, her bare feet making no sound on the silky antique rug. But it wasn't Leo; it was Dimitri who stood there and she de-spaired at the predictability of her reaction as the breath dried hotly in her throat.

'Is it Leo?' she questioned.

'No, Erin—it isn't Leo.' He glanced over her shoulder. 'You weren't in bed?'

'Not yet.' She was grateful for the darkness, which hid her sudden blush. And for the night-dress, which concealed her rapidly hardening nipples. 'I was just about to turn in.'

'May I come in?'

She didn't ask him why and that was her first

mistake. Her second was not to move away when he shut the door behind him. To get as far away from the intoxicating closeness of his body as the dimensions of the room would allow.

She tried to match the studied politeness he'd been showing her all day, but suddenly she noticed a new restlessness in his eyes. A certain tension in his powerful body. 'What is it that you want, Dimitri?'

She was trying to sound matter-of-fact but she failed miserably and something about the thready quality of her voice made his eyes narrow.

'I've come to say some things which I should have said a long time ago.'

She looked at him. 'What kind of things?'

Dimitri met the question in her green eyes and hesitated, because what he was about to do did not come easily to him. He had grown up in a world where explanations were never given, where feelings were buried so deeply that you could almost fool yourself into thinking they didn't exist. And he had carried on that same sterile tradition into his own adult life. *Never explain* had been his motto. People could take him as they found him and if they didn't like him, then tough. There were plenty more eager to fall into line, because power made people eager to please you.

But not Erin. Erin was different. She did what she thought was right—no matter at what cost to herself. And she was the mother of his child. She deserved his respect—he realised that now. And maybe she also needed to know some of the things he was fast discovering about himself.

'I understand now why you kept Leo from me for so long,' he said.

Her eyes were wary. 'You do?'

He nodded. 'Why would you want an innocent child being corrupted by someone who saw life through the bottom of a glass, as I did? Whose idea of fun was being the last person left in the casino after he'd emptied his wallet? Who revelled in the sense of danger, as much as the thrill of risk? I don't blame you for cutting me out of his life, because that's what any good mother would do and you are a fantastic mother,' he said slowly. 'And our son is beautiful. He's just beautiful, Erin.'

Erin didn't know what she'd been expecting, but this hadn't even featured on her list of possibilities. And the crazy thing was that the things he'd said made her want to cry. She found herself wishing he'd come and found her a long time ago to tell her he had cleaned up his act and then he could have met Leo a whole lot sooner. She thought of all those wasted years which they could never get back and suddenly she didn't want to risk a moment's more regret.

She blinked away the incipient tears which were pricking at the backs of her eyes. 'Kiss me,' she whispered.

'Erin—'

'Shut up,' she interrupted and in the midst of her hunger and heartache she realised that she was one of the few people he would *allow* to interrupt him like that. 'Just shut up and kiss me, Dimitri. Please.'

He moved forward and cupped her face in his hands and suddenly he was driving his mouth down onto hers, his tongue coaxing her lips apart as he began to explore her with an urgency which made her feel weak. She wondered if it was her self-imposed embargo on sex which made this kiss seem so...*profound*, or because it was underpinned by a distinct air of reconciliation?

She didn't know and, right now, she didn't care. The only thing she cared about was the way he was touching her—running the flat of his hand down over her flower-sprigged nightdress.

'Is this what the English call a passion-killer?' he questioned drily as he peeled off her long nightdress.

'Why?' She shivered as the cool air hit her heated skin. 'Is it working?'

'Are you kidding? It's the sexiest piece of clothing I've ever seen,' he growled as he picked her up and carried her over to the bed.

She helped him undress—her inexperience forgotten in the midst of her excitement at revealing the powerful body. She traced her fingers experimentally over his hair-roughened thighs, feeling stupidly pleased by his exultant shiver and the little groan of satisfaction he made. And wasn't that the thing about Dimitri—that somehow, despite everything, she always felt like his equal in bed?

The sheets felt cool against her naked body but Dimitri was all welcoming warmth as the mattress dipped beneath them. Tilting her chin, he looked at her for one long, wordless moment before slowly lowering his mouth to kiss her.

He wrapped his arms around her—his powerful legs entwining with hers and his fingers stroking her skin, so that at first she shivered and then relaxed. It felt so good to be here with him like this. Unbearably good. She found herself praying that he wouldn't hurt her—before vowing that she wouldn't ever *allow* herself to get hurt.

His hands moved to her hips, urging her even closer, and her nipples grew hard against his chest. She could feel the heavy weight of his erection pushing against her belly and her face grew hot. The blood in her veins seemed to be growing thicker. She could feel the molten heat between her legs and when he slid his fingers there, she writhed with pleasure—moving her body against him in a silent message of invitation.

'You like that, don't you, *milaya moya*?' he whispered and when she nodded eagerly, he whispered into her ear. 'Then *tell* me.'

'I…love it,' she whispered shakily. 'You know I do.'

Somehow he found a condom but his hands were unsteady as he slid it on, before entering her with such exquisite precision that Erin gasped.

He moved slowly at first—as if he had all the time in the world. And wasn't that exactly what it felt like? That for once there were no constraints, or questions. That she could simply enjoy this for what it was.

She was aware that his eyes were open and she felt confident enough to hold his gaze as each thrust took her higher. Every time he moved it increased her pleasure—tightening it, notch by delicious notch. And just when it became almost unbearable her orgasm hit her in waves so powerful that it felt as if it were tearing her body apart. Her fingers tightened around him as he shuddered inside her with a ragged groan of his own.

It seemed like ages before he withdrew and Erin had to fight the urge to claw at him—wanting to bring him back inside her. She turned to look at him. His eyes were closed and he appeared to be sleeping—and she knew him well enough to realise that he'd probably like her to turn over and go to sleep, too. She remembered once overhearing him saying to his friend Ivan: *The trouble with women is that they ask too many questions.*

For a long time she had tried to abide by his preferred diktat, because she'd wanted to be the perfect secretary. She had questioned him only when absolutely necessary—but those days were gone. Even if the intimacy they'd just shared didn't give her any rights—surely the fact that they had a son between them allowed her the luxury of asking questions for once. Wasn't it time he told her stuff—instead of making out that it was presumptuous of her to dare ask?

'Dimitri?'

'Mmm?'

'I want to ask you something.'

He opened his eyes. 'Must you?'

She ignored that, positioning herself more comfortably on the pillows so that she was in the direct line of his cool gaze. 'You know when you were going off the rails?'

'What about it?'

'You just never told me why. What made you do it?'

'Does there have to be a reason, Erin?'

'I don't know. You tell me.'

He was so quiet for a moment that Erin wondered whether he was just going to ignore her question, when suddenly he started talking.

'It was a combination of factors,' he said. 'I was living in London—and that was the world I was inhabiting at the time.'

She rested her chin on his chest and looked up at him. 'What kind of world was that?'

He shrugged. 'The world of success—and excess. My company was doing better than I could have ever dreamed. Suddenly, I had more time. More money. More everything, really. Whatever I touched seemed to turn to gold. My stocks were touching the stratosphere. Women were throwing themselves at me—'

'How unbearable that must have been.'

'At first I can't deny that I enjoyed it,' he said, skating over her sarcasm. 'But it doesn't take long for an appetite to become jaded. For too much to become not nearly enough. Suddenly, nothing ever seemed to *satisfy* me. I tried gambling, and then vodka. But nothing seemed to do it. Nothing could take away…'

His voice trailed off as if he'd said too much but Erin was onto it in an instant.

'Take away what?'

'It doesn't matter.'

'It *does* matter,' she said stubbornly.

His voice hardened. 'The discoveries I had made. The ones which made oblivion seem like a good idea.'

'What kind of discoveries?' she persisted.

'Erin, is this really relevant? We've just had some pretty amazing sex…' he trailed his finger down over her torso until it came to rest comfortably in her belly button '…and now you're ruining it by hurling all these questions at me.'

'How can talking ruin what's just happened?' She pushed his finger away. 'And it *is* relevant. It isn't just prurient curiosity on my part, if that's what you're thinking. It's about a need to know more about my son's heritage—so I don't have to look at him blankly when he asks me the questions he will one day inevitably ask. Because I want to be able to tell Leo the truth from now on.'

'I don't think these are the kind of things you'd want to tell an innocent young boy,' he said bitterly.

'But I'm a grown woman,' she said. 'You can tell me.'

Dimitri stared into her green eyes, thinking how catlike they looked against her flushed skin. Her dark hair was tumbling over her tiny breasts and every instinct in his body was urging him to block her questions and make love to her again. But some of her words were stubbornly refusing to shift. Didn't matter how much he wanted them to go away; they weren't going to. Because she was right. As the mother of his child didn't she *deserve* to hear the truth?

He gave an expansive flick of his hand—as if to draw attention to the dimensions of the huge room in which they lay. 'You can see for yourself how privileged my background was. I was the only son of a hugely successful businessman and his devoted wife.' He gave a bitter laugh. 'Or that's what I thought I was—until the whole pack of cards came tumbling down.'

For once she was silent, but he felt her grow very still beside him.

'I discovered that my life was nothing but an illusion based on lies and deception,' he said. 'It was all smoke and mirrors and nothing was as it seemed. My father wasn't the respectable businessman I'd always thought. His respectability was just a front for his underworld dealings. He made the bulk of his money from drugs and gambling, and from human trafficking and misery.'

He could see her eyes widening in shock, but he forced himself to continue—as if suddenly recognising the burden of having kept this to himself for all these years. Because wasn't that another legacy of criminality—that the secrets it created tainted everyone around with the sense of nothing being as it should be?

'My relationship with him wasn't good. He was the coldest man I've ever encountered. Sometimes I used to wonder if it was just something inside him which made him so distant—or whether it was something to do with *me*. I wondered why he sometimes looked through me as if I was invisible, or worse. As if he actually *hated* me.' He paused. 'It took a long time for me to discover why.'

'Why?'

He could hear her holding her breath.

'Because he wasn't actually my father,' he said slowly. 'I was the cuckoo child. A product of a passionate liaison between my mother and the family gardener.'

'Your mother had an affair with the *gardener*?'

He nodded and waited while she processed this piece of information.

'And what was he like? This gardener.'

Dimitri frowned. He had been anticipating judgement—not understanding. Was it that which made him stray deeper into the memory—into the dark place he usually kept locked and bolted?

'A striking man,' he said slowly. 'Tall and muscular, with tawny hair and blue eyes. I remember how much the maids used to idolise him and how women turned to look at him whenever he walked by. But most of all, he was kind. I didn't realise that men could be kind. It never occurred to me to question why he used to spend so much time with me—way more than my father ever did. It didn't even occur to me until much later that whenever I looked at him, it was like looking in the mirror. But afterwards I wished he'd said something—something to acknowledge that I was his. But he never did.' He saw how wide her green eyes had grown. 'Shocked, Erin?'

'Not half as shocked as you must have been.' She seemed to choose her next words with care. 'But if your other father knew you weren't his child, then why did he stay with your mother? Why didn't he just divorce her and cut his losses?'

'And lose face?' Dimitri gave a hollow laugh. 'Admit that some *labourer* had succeeded where he had failed? No. That wasn't the way he operated. My mother's punishment was to remain in a loveless marriage. Locked in a relationship based on fear with a man who despised her. And I think she felt the same way about me. I can certainly never remember her being warm towards me.' He sucked in a breath. 'Maybe she didn't dare show me affection because she knew it would enrage my father. Or maybe she saw me as a constant reminder of what she had done. Maybe I represented the failure she'd made of her life and her relationships.'

'And the gardener? What happened to him?'

There was a long silence before he shrugged. 'One morning he just wasn't there any more. I remember it was winter and the front door was open and I went looking for my mother. I found her in the forest, in the little shed where he used to keep his tools. She was curled up on the floor crying her eyes out, half mad with grief.'

'And did you...' Erin's hand crept over his and squeezed it. 'Did you ever meet up with him again? Did you ever form some kind of relationship and make peace with the past?'

His eyes were icier than she'd ever seen them—

and that was saying something about a man who could do every degree of ice.

'No,' he said abruptly. 'Although I tried. After my mother died I attempted to track him and that was when I discovered that he had been executed some years before.'

'Executed?'

'Killed by a single bullet to the head in a Moscow alleyway. It was, as they say in the business, a professional hit.'

'And you think...' She licked her lips. 'You think your father was behind it?'

'I'm no longer a gambling man,' he said, but she saw the awful knowledge written in his eyes.

Erin squeezed his hand tighter as she began to understand why he'd wanted to escape from the reality of his past. Because he had said himself that everyone was a product of their own experience. And Dimitri's was darker than most. His was the kind of past which kept psychiatrists in business. A mother who didn't show her love and a cold-hearted crook who hated you because you weren't his son. A crook who had probably ordered an execution, thus effectively cutting off any opportunity for reconciliation between Dimitri and his real father. Was it any wonder that he'd gone off the rails quite so spectacularly?

She rested her head against his shoulder, even though she wanted to do so much more. She wanted to hug him tightly and tell him everything was going to be all right. She wanted to cover his golden face with kisses and tell him she was there for him and would always be there for him, if only he would let her. But some instinct stopped her. She reminded herself that she didn't *do* emotional stuff like that and, more important, neither did he. Yet it was hard to restrain her instinct to reach out to him and it left her feeling confused.

She told herself that what she was feeling was just natural sympathy after hearing a particularly grim story. Except that it wasn't—because it felt like something more. Something which she'd tried to convince herself was the biggest con in the world and one she was never going to fall for again.

She swallowed as she turned her face away from his.

It felt uncomfortably like love.

CHAPTER ELEVEN

NOW WHAT?

Dimitri glanced across the room to where Leo was teaching Erin how to play the popular card game of P'yanitsa. A game the boy hadn't known how to play until earlier that week, but he was a quick learner—and now he was playing it as well as any Russian. Dimitri felt a stir of pride whisper over him as he studied the bent head of dark gold—so like his own—as once again the question nagged at him.

What was he going to do about the problem of a small boy and a woman who talked more than was comfortable?

His eyes moved to the woman in question as he watched Erin smiling as Leo scooped up a handful of cards with a triumphant whoop. To look at her now—you would never have guessed that a few hours ago he had been deep inside her while the rest of the house still slept. She had ridden him as he had shown her how he liked to be ridden, his hands on either side of her hips as he had positioned her to make penetration even deeper. And afterwards she had choked out her sigh as his tongue had slid down over her and he'd tasted her flesh.

'You must learn to be a good sport, darling,' she was saying softly. 'And to play fair.'

Play fair. It wouldn't have been the lesson Dimitri would have focused on. In fact, up until a week ago, he would have said the opposite—that playing fair never got you anywhere. That in the big, harsh world out there, it was dog eat dog. But now he could see that you shouldn't teach a child to cut corners, or to operate ruthlessly. He understood that you needed to show them how to do things right in order for them to live right. Just because his own childhood had been messed up, that was no reason for him to try to impose his own cynicism on someone else.

And Erin had shown him that—by example rather than preaching. She was patient and understanding with Leo—pretty much every minute of every day—and Dimitri knew with a heavy certainty that he could never be the instrument to drive the two of them apart. His heart pounded. Because hadn't that been a consideration when he'd first found out about Leo—thinking he might be able to lure the boy away using the power of his wealth and influence? He'd planned to show the child that he could have more fun in penthouses and private jets than he ever could living in the cramped quarters above his aunt's café. But that option wasn't on the cards any more—and it made him uncomfortable to think he could have ever entertained such a ruthless strategy.

He stared out of the window, where the grey skies were heavy with snow and the occasional stray flake drifted past like a white feather. But experience told him that the snow would not fall tonight and it looked as if Leo wouldn't get his snowman, no matter how hard he wished for it. Tomorrow they were flying back to England because half-term was almost over and Dimitri knew he needed to come to some sort of decision about what was going to happen.

He waited until Leo had gone through his bedtime routine and, once he'd been embraced in a sleepy bear hug, Dimitri went downstairs to wait for Erin in the library while she read a bedtime story.

He lit a fire, which crackled magnificently—the light from the flames flickering over the rows of books which lined the room, while Shostakovich played in the background. He spoke to Svetlana and soon two crystal flutes were standing beside a bottle in an ice bucket, but Erin's footsteps were so quiet that he didn't realise she was in the room until she was standing right in front of him.

She had changed and brushed her hair, so that

it gleamed like a dark waterfall around her shoulders, and a soft woollen dress was hugging her slender hips. He noticed that she frowned slightly when she saw the bottle standing on the table next to the peach blossom bonsai tree.

'Champagne?' she said lightly. 'Why, are we celebrating something?'

'I don't know.' He lifted the bottle from the ice bucket and cold droplets slid onto his fingers. 'At least, not yet.'

'Is this some sort of guessing game?'

'Do you want to try guessing?'

'Okay.' She screwed up her face. 'We're celebrating a successful trip?'

'That's one thing we could drink to, I agree. It has been a very successful trip.' He peeled away the foil and let it flutter to the table. 'Which is why I think we should get married.'

Erin stared at him.

'Did you say *married*—just out of the blue like that?'

'Why not?' There was a hissing little pop as he eased the cork from the bottle. 'What do you say?'

What did she say? Erin swallowed. She didn't have a clue how to respond. She felt perplexed— and bewildered. This had come out of nowhere with no warning whatsoever. And now he was pouring champagne, which was fizzing up the sides of a flute so delicate she was terrified her shaking hand might snap off its fragile stem. She shook her head as he held the flute out towards her.

'Not right now, thanks. This has come as a bit of a shock,' she said, aware of the glaring under-statement in her words. She tried to rid her voice of any hope or expectation. 'I mean, *why*? Why do you want to marry me, Dimitri?'

'You don't know?'

'If I knew, I wouldn't have to ask.'

He smiled. 'Because of Leo, of course.'

Of course.

Erin nodded. The logical part of her brain had known that all along but that didn't protect her from the sudden stupid lurch of disappointment which chilled her skin. And she didn't want to be *disappointed*. She wanted to be cool and calm and impartial. Just like him. She wanted to treat a proposal of marriage with the same kind of careless interest as it had been offered. 'And how would that work?' she said.

'Isn't it obvious?'

'Not to me, no. I'm not in the habit of getting random proposals of marriage from men who only a short time ago were barely able to look at me without being furious. You'll have to talk me through it.'

He turned the swell of music down by a fraction and one of the logs in the fireplace spat out a shoal of bright sparks. 'You must realise that I've grown very fond of Leo.'

She nodded. 'That's good.'

'And I consider you an excellent mother. I told you that.'

'Again, that's very good. But neither of these facts are reasons enough for us to get married, Dimitri.'

'No, they aren't. But there are other considerations, too. Financially you cannot deny that you struggle, while, fortunately, I do not. And my wealth could help make both your lives considerably more comfortable.'

She tried to smile. 'You realise you don't have to put a gold band on my finger in order to pay maintenance?'

The second movement of the concerto came to a finish and the fire spat again—a hissing and angry sound this time.

'Damn you, Erin Turner.' Dimitri's words fell softly and fervently into the short silence which followed. 'Do you really want me to spell this out for you?'

She met his eyes. 'I'm afraid you're going to have to.'

'It's more than just about the money. I want to be *there* for him,' he said, his voice growing deep, and passionate. 'To be there for the ordinary things—not just the high days and holidays. I want grumpy mornings as well as Christmas morning. I want to be hands-on—not absent for most of the time. To give him what I never had.'

Erin stared at him as a bubble of hope began to rise inside her—even though she was doing everything in her power not to get ahead of herself. In case it was futile. In case it hurt her in a way she'd vowed she would never let herself get hurt. 'And you would marry me in order to achieve that?'

'Yes,' he said emphatically. 'I would. Because I've come to realise that you are the perfect woman for me.'

Erin blinked because now hope was refusing to listen to her reservations. It was hurtling through her body like a runaway train and flattening everything in its track. 'I am?'

His icy eyes glittered. 'Indeed you are. I like the way that you don't try to manipulate me or covet my money, or possessions.' He paused. 'And, of course, you drive me wild in bed. Wilder than I ever thought possible, *zvezda moya*.'

'And that's enough?'

'No, it is not. But you have another attribute which is rare. So rare that I have never found it before. The silver bullet, if you like—which is that you don't love me. You don't believe in love. Well, neither do I.' He smiled. 'Now, isn't that just a match made in heaven?'

Her knees went weak and Erin only just managed to stop herself from crumpling as she listened to his cruel parody of a marriage proposal. Everything a man was traditionally supposed to say at a time like this, he had twisted round. He had made dark what was supposed to be light. He had projected a future which would make their proposed union into nothing but a *mockery*. A pastiche of a marriage, which would be little better than the one which had ruined his own life.

'And you think that's the kind of example I want to set my son?' she questioned, her voice trembling with a hurt she could no longer hide. 'That I want him growing up with two people who are proud of never experiencing an emotion which has driven the human race since the beginning of time?'

'I didn't say I was proud of it.'

'I don't care what you said,' she hissed, aware that her sense of logic was haemorrhaging by the second.

'And I don't understand either your outrage or your objections,' he snapped. 'You were happy enough to marry Chico for financial security, weren't you? When we both know he wasn't offering you half the benefits you could get from me.'

'You're disgusting,' she snapped as she heard the unmistakable sexual allusion which had roughened his voice. Did he really think *that* could sway her? That his skill between the sheets would make her forget all her principles? She shook her head. 'I don't need a heartless man to bankroll the life I want for Leo and me. I can achieve what I need all by myself, Dimitri, and what's more—I'm going to. There's nothing to stop us moving out of London and going to live in a cheaper part of England. There's a whole lot of beautiful countryside just waiting out there.'

'But think how much easier it would be with me behind you.'

'But that's where you're completely wrong.' She shook her head as she stared at him, aware of the crackling fire and the heavy beat of her heart. 'Because I've suddenly discovered a fundamental flaw in my own argument.'

'I don't understand,' he said coldly.

Maybe because she was only just beginning to understand herself. She sucked in a deep breath, realising that she was laying everything on the line here. But why run from the truth any more? Surely it was better to feel *something* rather than nothing. To live rather than to exist. Because Dimitri had been right about one thing and that was that you couldn't protect yourself against being hurt. That being hurt was part of life itself.

'I thought I didn't believe in love,' she said slowly. 'But the irony is that somewhere along the way I've fallen in love with you, Dimitri.

I didn't want to. I still don't want to—because you're the last man in the world any sane woman would choose to be in love with. You're cold and you're heartless and you don't give out your trust very easily. But don't they say that the heart takes no prisoners? I started loving you a long time ago, and, no matter how hard I've tried to get you out of my system, it seems that none of my methods have worked.' She gave a wry smile. 'Oh, don't worry—I'm not asking you to reciprocate, because I realise you can't. But obviously I can't marry you under these circumstances. It wouldn't be fair—not to you, nor to me and especially not to Leo.'

'Why not?'

'Because unrequited love doesn't work,' she said impatiently. 'It's a recipe for disaster—everyone knows that! And love doesn't really last. All the books say it changes once all that new sex wears off.'

'But hasn't your parents' love affair lasted?'

She glared at him, wondering why he was trying to argue for something he didn't believe in. Was it just because he always liked to win? She stared at the two glasses of champagne, which had now stopped fizzing. 'They are the exception which proves the rule,' she said quietly. 'And they're ordinary people—not oligarchs. My father doesn't have women throwing themselves at him every minute of the day, like you do. You're only objecting because I'm not doing what you want me to do. But the reality is that you'll grow bored with me and start looking round for someone younger and prettier—and I couldn't bear that. I'm just being realistic and facing facts, because falling in love doesn't mean I've had part of my brain removed. I'm doing you a favour, Dimitri. I'm not going to limit your time with Leo—in fact, I'll do everything in my power to make sure you see as much of him as you want. But I'm not going to marry you. Do you understand?'

CHAPTER TWELVE

DAMN HER.

Just *damn* her.

Dimitri glowered. He would not… He would *not* be emotionally blackmailed.

He studied the antique bowl containing the grouping of bonsai trees which adorned the polished desk of his London office—an exquisite planting of seven Foemina Junipers, which had been created by a Japanese master. It had taken a lot for Dimitri to persuade the man to sell it, because he had needed convincing that the trees would be properly cared for and kept in the right conditions. It had occurred to Dimitri at the time that the plants' welfare had been of far greater concern to the master than the astronomical price tag which accompanied it.

Usually, just staring at the priceless piece of horticulture brought him some kind of peace, but not today. He studied the bowl. The idea that something as enormous as a tree could be clipped and contained into a size small enough to keep on a man's desk had always appealed to his dark sense of humour. But he realised that he also enjoyed the element of control essential for successful bonsai care. Conditions needed to be monitored daily, with nothing left to chance. Any sign of rampant growth needed to be ruthlessly cut away. It was man controlling nature. And it was a representation of how he liked to live his life.

Until now.

Now he was discovering that not everything could be controlled. With a heavy sigh he sat back in his chair and thought about Erin. She had meant it when she'd turned down his proposal of marriage. He couldn't quite believe it at first, but she had. There had been no wavering or sign she might be softening—not during the flight back from Moscow or the journey at the other end, when he'd dropped her and Leo off at the café.

She had made him feel…

What?

He swallowed. She had made him feel powerless. For the first time in a long time, he had come up against someone who would not be moulded to his formidable will, no matter how many enticements he offered her.

He had tried telling himself she was right. Much better that he had as much contact with his son without risking the messy emotional fallout of sharing his life with another person. He'd returned from Russia determined to seek his pleasure elsewhere and had flicked through the stack of invitations which were waiting for him.

But all he could think about was a pair of green eyes and a woman who only smiled when she wanted to.

He thought about the things she'd said and his eyes focused on the Foemina Junipers again. Had she been trying to tell him that the conditions essential for maintaining a successful marriage needed to be right, just as with the bonsai? Just as you couldn't grow a tiny tree in barren soil, neither could a relationship flourish properly without love and care and commitment? Was that what she had meant?

Damn her.

He waited two days for her to change her mind and come running and he waited in vain. His days seemed drawn-out and tedious and the nights were even worse. He hadn't slept this badly since the time he'd cut out vodka. Saturday morning dawned and, after a largely sleepless night, he drove himself round to the café, where he sat outside the citrus-decked exterior in his big car—half expecting Erin to come storming out and demand to know what he was doing there. Or perhaps send Leo out to talk to him, because wouldn't that have been an easy way to break the stand-off which had sprung up between them?

But nobody came. He could see her sister behind the counter—her eyes big behind her owl-like spectacles—but she didn't wave at him to come in.

He got out of the car and locked it, his heart pounding as he pushed open the café door. It was warm and crowded with customers, with mothers and fathers and little children as well as a couple wearing party clothes who didn't appear to have been to bed. Several people looked up as the jangling bell announced his arrival, and stayed looking.

Walking straight over to the counter, he smiled at the woman who stood there, drying coffee cups.

'It's Tara, isn't it?' he said. 'I'm Dimitri.'

'I know who you are,' she said flatly. 'And Leo's at Saturday morning football, I'm afraid.'

'It isn't Leo I've come to see. It's Erin.'

There was a slight pause as she looked around before lowering her voice, as if she didn't want to put her livelihood at risk by engaging in some kind of showdown with the tall man who had just walked into her café.

'Erin doesn't want to see you.'

'Well, I'm not leaving here until she does. So perhaps you'd like to pour me a cup of coffee and I'll wait over there while you tell her that? Black, no sugar, please.'

Tara's mouth opened and closed, before she disappeared into the back behind some sort of curtain and Dimitri walked over to a table near the window and sat down. A woman who was sitting on her own at a nearby table smiled at him, but he didn't smile back. He didn't feel like smiling—least of all to some bottle blonde who might as well have had the word 'available' tattooed across her forehead.

A shadow fell over the table and he looked up to see Erin standing there. Over her jeans and sweater, she was wearing an apron which emphasised her tiny waist—but she didn't look great. In fact, she looked terrible. Her face was pale and her green eyes were dark and shadowed.

'Perhaps you'd like to drag your attention away

from that woman for a moment,' she said tightly, 'and tell me what you're doing here?'

'You haven't brought my coffee.'

'You're not getting any coffee.' Pulling out the chair opposite him, she sat down and leaned across the table and began speaking in a low voice. 'Look, you're welcome to come and see Leo any time you want—I already told you that—but you really have to give me some warning before you do. I can't just have you turning up here out of the blue like this.'

'Why not?'

'You know why not. Because it's too…disturbing. We have to try to learn to be…' She hesitated. 'I don't know. If not exactly *friends*, then certainly two parents who can interact amicably with each other.'

He nodded, his eyes not leaving her face. 'But I thought we *were* friends, Erin. More than friends. Don't you know that I'm closer to you than I've ever been to anyone else?'

'I don't want to hear this—'

'And let me tell you something else,' he interrupted. 'Something I've never told you before. Something which happened when you came round to my apartment, to tell me about the baby.'

'You mean when I found you hungover, with the naked woman and the porn films?'

'And you looked down your nose at me,' he said slowly. 'Just like you're trying to do now, only this time you aren't making such a good job of it. But back then you didn't like what you saw and you told me so in no uncertain terms. You told me a lot of home truths that day, Erin. You blasted me and my lifestyle and left me feeling dazed. Because nobody had ever spoken to me like that before. And then you handed in your notice and walked away.'

'I don't understand what this has to do with anything,' she said. 'We already know this.'

'But you don't know what I did next,' he said. 'At first I tried to convince myself I was glad you'd gone and that you had no right to judge me. But I couldn't stop thinking about the things you'd said. And the more I thought about them, the more I realised they were true. You left me feeling bad about myself and I had to ask myself what I was intending to do about it. So I went away and cleaned up my act. I quit the booze and the gambling and the women.' He saw her face and shrugged. 'Well, maybe not all the women, but I started to be more discriminating about it. And I got off that merry-go-round of self-destruction you'd highlighted so accurately.' He leaned across the table towards her. 'You were the catalyst which made me examine my life and turn it around. So I owe you, Erin. I owe you big-time.'

'Thanks very much. And if you want my congratulations, then you have them—but I still don't see why you're bringing all this up now.'

'Don't you? Though why should you when I've only just realised myself? When it's taken me all this time to admit what's been staring me in the face for so long. That you've had a profound and lasting influence on me.' He waited for a minute and then drew a deep breath. 'That I love you—and I don't want to spend my life without you in it.'

She didn't answer, not at first—just nodded her head. 'Dimitri,' she said at last, sounding as if she was trying desperately to keep her voice from breaking. 'Listen to me. I'm not going to change my mind about marrying you—so please don't say things you don't mean.'

'But I *do* mean it. Every word I speak straight from here.' And he placed his hand over his heart.

'Will you stop it?' she hissed. 'Everybody's looking at us.'

'I don't care.' He took her left hand between his palms and thought how cold her fingers felt. How stiff her body language was as she sat there facing him. 'Just tell me that it's not too late,' he said. 'Tell me that you still love me—as you did that night in Russia. Tell me that you'll marry me and spend the rest of your life with me.'

Erin was aware that pretty much everyone in the café knew what was happening. Even if they couldn't hear—and Dimitri was making no attempt whatsoever to lower his voice—then it was now glaringly obvious, because he was digging into the pocket of his suit jacket and pulling out a small box.

He flipped open the lid and she could see the dazzle as the light caught the glittering band of diamonds in the centre of which was one enormous and flawless stone, and from behind the counter she heard Tara gasp.

'I have had this ring fashioned from the very finest diamonds in my mine,' he said. 'But if it's too big or too flashy, we can get you something else. We could buy you something antique and special in Moscow or Paris, if that's what you'd prefer. I'd just like you to wear it in the meantime, because I want to see it on your finger. Because ironically, despite having run all my life from matrimony, I have now become its greatest advocate. That is…' he stared at her '…if you'll agree to marry me?'

Erin saw the flicker of uncertainty in his eyes—so brief that she might have imagined it—

and somehow it made her love him even more. Dimitri uncertain? Whoever would have thought it? It was something as impossible to imagine as him making such a public and romantic proposal in an East End café. She had tried to stop loving him, but somehow it just wouldn't work and now she had accepted that it was never going to. He was complicated, there was no doubt about that. He was brilliant at some things but not so good at others. Feelings and emotion, mainly… those were the things he liked to hide away—at least until now. But now she understood why. And didn't he need her love just as badly as she wanted to give it? 'Oh, Dimitri,' she whispered. 'Of course I'll marry you. I—'

But her words were drowned out by his laugh of pleasure as he rose to his feet and walked round to her side of the table, where he lifted her to her feet. He stared into her face for what seemed like a long time before he started to kiss her, and all the customers—except for the blonde—burst into a spontaneous round of clapping and cheering.

In the commotion, the ring fell to the ground and remained missing until Leo and his friends came back from football later that morning, crawling around on their hands and knees until it was located underneath the skirting board. They were rewarded with ice cream and cola and the promise of a trip to watch Chelsea play, and Erin overheard Leo saying to his best friend, 'That's my *daddy*.'

She blinked a little at that, because she didn't actually remember telling him that. And that was when it all became real and tears of happiness began to slide down her cheeks.

EPILOGUE

LEO GOT HIS snowman after all—along with sleigh bells and fairy lights and the realisation that having a Russian father and an English mother meant he could actually celebrate *two* Christmases, instead of one. The first was spent in England, with Dimitri flying Erin's parents in from Australia as a surprise and Tara closing down the café for a whole fortnight. Dimitri booked an entire floor of the Granchester Hotel for the festivities, which famously had the biggest tree in London—if you didn't count the one in Trafalgar Square.

And somewhere amid all the excitement, they got married. They exchanged their vows and, for those heartfelt moments, felt like the only two people in the world. Outside, the ground glittered with frost and Erin wore a hooded white cashmere cloak over her long, silk dress. With Leo at her side as proud ring bearer, she carried camomile daisies—the national flower of Russia—mixed with white freesia, which were her mother's favourites. Chico was invited but had flown back to Brazil to tell his parents he was gay and no longer intended to live a lie. Saladin was also invited but his favourite and most valuable horse was injured and he was at his wits' end.

Their second Christmas of the year was spent in Russia, where the holiday was traditionally celebrated on January the seventh and nothing was eaten all day, until the first star had been seen in the sky, when a dish called *kutia* was taken from a shared bowl, to signify unity. And if once upon a time Leo would have turned his nose up at the thought of walnut-and-fruit-studded porridge, he dug into the dish with enthusiasm as the three of them ate their meal together.

Erin remembered staring at her son in amazement, and thinking how much he'd changed.

How much they'd all changed.

Leo had blossomed beneath the warm glow of his father's love—a love which Dimitri had confessed he wasn't sure he'd be able to show, just as he wasn't sure if he was capable of being a good father. Erin guessed that wasn't surprising, because if you'd never been properly fathered when you were a little boy, then how would you know how it worked? But Dimitri had worked it out. Of course he had. Her cold, proud Russian had melted—morphing into a man with so much love to give that it made her heart sing just to think about it.

She'd changed, too. The dark fears and insecurities which had nudged the corners of her soul were now a thing of the past. She recognised that it was more than Dimitri's love which had helped her to accomplish that. It was finding her own inner strength and conviction. She'd been strong enough to tell him that she wouldn't settle for second best. To show him that she could and would live independently, even if that was the harder option. Sometimes you needed to be prepared to walk away from the thing you most wanted, in order to get it to come to you.

She lay back against the sofa while the fire crackled and waited while Dimitri read Leo a bedtime story. He would be down in a minute and tomorrow they were taking him and Anatoly sleighing. And after that they would probably build yet *another* snowman.

She sighed.

'Such a very big sigh,' Dimitri observed softly as he walked into the room and the light from the crackling fire turned his hair red-gold.

'A happy sigh.'

'Oh?'

She looked up at him as he joined her on the sofa, his arm sliding around her back, and automatically she snuggled up to him. 'I was just thinking how lucky I am. Lucky to have met you and had your baby. Lucky to be with you now.'

He looked down at her very intently as he brushed the hair away from her face. 'And all the in-between years? The wasted years?'

She shook her head. 'No, not that. I've been thinking about that and they definitely weren't wasted. They were learning years. Growing years—and growing is always painful. Unless of course you happen to be a bonsai tree, in which case you don't even get the chance!'

He smiled. 'Any ideas what you'd like to do tonight?'

'Surprise me.'

His smile deepened as he cupped her face in his hands and moved his own close enough for her to feel the warmth of his breath.

'I'm going to pour you a glass of champagne and tell you how much I love you, before thrashing you at P'yanitsa.'

'A busy schedule,' she observed.

'Very busy,' he agreed as his lips brushed over hers. 'And after that…'

'After that…what?' she questioned breathlessly as his fingertips brushed over her breast.

'On second thoughts,' he said roughly, 'maybe the P'yanitsa can wait…'

* * * * *

MILLS & BOON®
Large Print – February 2016

Claimed for Makarov's Baby
Sharon Kendrick

An Heir Fit for a King
Abby Green

The Wedding Night Debt
Cathy Williams

Seducing His Enemy's Daughter
Annie West

Reunited for the Billionaire's Legacy
Jennifer Hayward

Hidden in the Sheikh's Harem
Michelle Conder

Resisting the Sicilian Playboy
Amanda Cinelli

Soldier, Hero...Husband?
Cara Colter

Falling for Mr December
Kate Hardy

The Baby Who Saved Christmas
Alison Roberts

A Proposal Worth Millions
Sophie Pembroke

0116 Rom LP

MILLS & BOON®
Large Print – March 2016

A Christmas Vow of Seduction
Maisey Yates

Brazilian's Nine Months' Notice
Susan Stephens

The Sheikh's Christmas Conquest
Sharon Kendrick

Shackled to the Sheikh
Trish Morey

Unwrapping the Castelli Secret
Caitlin Crews

A Marriage Fit for a Sinner
Maya Blake

Larenzo's Christmas Baby
Kate Hewitt

His Lost-and-Found Bride
Scarlet Wilson

Housekeeper Under the Mistletoe
Cara Colter

Gift-Wrapped in Her Wedding Dress
Kandy Shepherd

The Prince's Christmas Vow
Jennifer Faye

MILLS & BOON®

Why shop at millsandboon.co.uk?

Each year, thousands of romance readers find their perfect read at millsandboon.co.uk. That's because we're passionate about bringing you the very best romantic fiction. Here are some of the advantages of shopping at www.millsandboon.co.uk:

* **Get new books first**—you'll be able to buy your favourite books one month before they hit the shops

* **Get exclusive discounts**—you'll also be able to buy our specially created monthly collections, with up to 50% off the RRP

* **Find your favourite authors**—latest news, interviews and new releases for all your favourite authors and series on our website, plus ideas for what to try next

* **Join in**—once you've bought your favourite books, don't forget to register with us to rate, review and join in the discussions

Visit **www.millsandboon.co.uk**
for all this and more today!

LJ/2017